Greed

SEVEN DEADLY SINS

Compiled & Edited by
Ben Thomas & D Kershaw

Also available from Black Hare Press
DARK DRABBLES ANTHOLOGIES

WORLDS
ANGELS
MONSTERS
BEYOND
UNRAVEL
APOCALYPSE
LOVE
HATE
OCEANS
ANCIENTS

BHP WRITERS' GROUP SPECIAL EDITIONS

STORMING AREA 51
EERIE CHRISTMAS
BAD ROMANCE
TWENTY TWENTY
SCHOOL'S IN

OTHER VOLUMES

DEEP SPACE
WHAT IF?
KEY TO THE KINGDOM
BEYOND THE REALM
DEEP SEA

Twitter: @BlackHarePress
Facebook: BlackHarePress
Website: www.BlackHarePress.com

Where Love's environs vanish, yours begin : Your black banditti guised
as traders hold The ports and opened routes of Peace: your bold And
sacrilegious hands part graveside kin From tears to factioned hate :
your baubles win Caressing Judas to his treason cold : And, alchemist
of virus into gold, You churn the ooze of every deadly sin.

Mephitic empires spread to fill your maw : And crowded Indigence,
with wan vice flecked, Her blotched toll yields your pitiless decree :
Your tempests wither Freedom, taint the law, Dismantle love to
whoredom, yea, have wrecked A Universal Church on Simony

None held his own, none knew his child before My fierce tabus and
jealous marriage ties ; No leaking vat escapes my prudent eyes : I glean
the sheaves To-day's full arms ignore To eke distraught To-morrow's
shrunken store : Temple and home from my gold basements rise : And
raw chaotic earth I humanize Pulsing arterial Trade from shore to shore.

I pile the hoards that manumit the slave, Shelter the widow and her
orphans well, Support the sower while the harvests sleep, And tempt
the modest master from his cell To paint a Sistlne sky, a Moses grave,
Or bid Renascent fires o'er Florence leap!

Avarice **by Bernard O'Dowd, 1909**

Table of Contents

Death and Taxes

by Tim Mendees

Sir Percy Eddleston the Third closed the heavy ledger, replaced his fountain pen in its wooden box, leaned back in his wingback chair, and grinned. The dim flickering light of the oil lamp gave him a sickly, cadaverous appearance as he directed his rictus towards the painting of Queen Victoria that hung over the mantel. It was rather fitting under the circumstances…

As the sole councillor for the parish of Betyls Cove, it was his duty to make sure that the meagre Royal Grant was spent where it was needed the most…in *his* back pocket. He had complete freedom to do pretty much whatever he liked. Nobody in the rest of England cared one jot as to what was happening in his poky little Cornish backwater, and the locals blindly went along with his *leadership*. God bless the "Local Government Act"!

Born with a streak of avarice wider than the English channel, Percy was always on the lookout for new and innovative ways to wring an extra shilling out of the populous… This one was a stroke of genius even if he said so himself. He already had the fanciest house in town, the fanciest clothes, and the fanciest wife, but that didn't stop him. There was always room for more wealth…

"Tax the dead…" he had hissed to himself as the metaphorical gas bulb popped above his balding head. His eyes twinkled behind his wire-framed spectacles as he had a sip of fine Cognac to get the brain machinery nicely oiled and firing on all cylinders. Replacing the glass on the mahogany desk and snipping the end off a fine cigar, Percy trembled with excitement. *How had I never thought of this before?* He thought to himself. *Tax the dead!*

It was an auspicious idea, some would say devilish, but he had been driven to it really. After all, death was the only growth industry in the area. The fishing industry was on the decline and tourism was at an all-time low. This coupled with the sobering fact that the local life expectancy rate was far lower than the nationwide average of 35 meant that the only people making any serious money were the undertakers.

The question was "How does one tax the dead?" Percy mulled it over as he alternated between sipping his brandy and puffing on his cigar. Then it hit him: *I'll charge them rent!* He would charge the deceased for ground rent on the graves, and as the dead can't pay him themselves, he would simply bill the next of kin. And if they couldn't settle the debt…the dead would be evicted like any bad tenant. To top it all, the church couldn't do a damned thing about it as he owned the land the cemetery was situated upon…*his* land, *his* rules…

As he chuckled to himself ghoulishly, one of his myriad of servants—a young local by the name of Connor Edwards—knocked on the study door. "Come!" Percy barked.

"Beggin' ye pardon, sir." Connor grovelled, doffing his peaked cap. "Mrs Emerson wondered if you'd be taking supper downstairs or in your chambers."

Percy puffed out his mutton chops and thought for a second. "Tell her that I'll be down in an hour… there's a good chap."

"Very well, sir," Connor replied with due deference.

As he backed out of the room with his head bowed, Percy had another flash of devious inspiration. "Hold on one moment, will you?"

"Sir?" Connor looked puzzled. The bluff old miser had barely said three words to him in the three years he had worked for him. "Can I help you with summat?"

"Sit down, lad." Percy motioned to the stool next to the shelving which housed his precious ledgers. "I wanted to ask you about your Uncle Rufous."

Connor gulped. The last time Percy mentioned Uncle

Rufous, it was when the sly old bugger had been caught poaching on Percy's estate... The fine was astronomical… Ten bob for a lousy rabbit! "Ugh…yes, sir?" Connor stammered with trepidation.

Percy fixed him with a knowing stare. "Does your uncle still talk to the *things* that live in the cemetery?"

Connor nearly choked. "I…don't know…wh…what you mean." He did…he knew only too well what his employer meant.

"Come, come." Percy flashed a vulturine smile. "Do you really think that I didn't know about his *friends* in the graveyard?" He puffed out his chest like a proud pigeon. "I know everything that happens in *my* town."

"Yes, sir… Sorry, sir," Connor mumbled as his cheeks burned with the flames of embarrassment. "What do you want to know, sir?"

"Does he have any…sway…with the creatures?" Percy took a thoughtful puff on his cigar for effect. "What I mean to say is, can he strike a bargain with them?"

"Bargain?" Connor blinked like a startled rabbit.

"Yes, a bargain. A deal…" Percy leaned closer to the trembling youth—so close, in fact, that his brandy breath burned the boy's retinas. "I hear that those *creatures* are corpse eaters…"

If Connor had possessed any inkling of Percy's grand

money-spinning scheme, he would probably have fled from the room screaming as the implication of this comment led to a disgusting revelation… Percy planned to feed the *evicted* dead to the corpse eaters that lived under the graveyard.

Connor nodded his understanding. "Yes, I think he is on good terms with the ghouls, sir."

"Ha!" Percy spluttered in amusement. "So that's what they call themselves, is it?" He chuckled so heartily that he choked on his cigar smoke; the corpulent fellow was lucky that he didn't rupture something. After a moment of compulsive coughing, he carried on. "Very well. I would like you to *invite* your uncle to supper tomorrow. Tell him that if he helps me, I may have a position for him as my gamekeeper. I'm sure that will tantalise the old devil." Percy winked. Connor shuddered.

Connor rose and scurried from the room after assuring his employer that he would do his level best to get his uncle to agree to a meeting. He was pretty sure that the offer of money would have been a far better incentive than the prospect of employment, but if Percy *had* offered money, Connor would probably have expired through shock…

Percy stubbed out his cigar and swilled back the last of the brandy before rubbing his clammy paws together… He could almost smell the money his new tax would reap…

"You don't expect me to go down there, do you?" Percy pointed in horror at the tunnel that had been revealed in a forlorn and forgotten corner of the cemetery. His guide, Rufous Edwards, had revealed the entrance by sweeping aside a tangled curtain of ivy. The smell of decay was overpowering.

"You don't expect them to turn up at one of yer fancy dinner parties, do you?" Rufous scoffed. "It's not like they can just go and get fitted for a suit, you know?"

Percy glared at his newly appointed gamekeeper. If only he didn't need him as an intermediary, he'd have raised the rents on his farmhouse and had him on the streets so fast that his head would have spun. "Very well," he grumbled sullenly. "But I don't see why I have to talk to the foul creatures. That was supposed to be your job." He pointed a stubby finger at Rufous.

Rufous smirked under his shaggy beard. "Nay, sir. Our agreement was that I cut a deal with the ghoulies. It ain't my fault that they wanted you to sign the papers in front of them as part of the bargain, is it?" In fact, it was. He wanted to make damn sure that he knew exactly *who* he was dealing with. It was his suggestion that Edwards go down into their lair. A suggestion that the elder of the pack saw would be greatly beneficial… Even below ground, Percy was known as a man that was not to be trusted.

Percy knew that he had been outmanoeuvred by the wily poacher, but he had little choice other than to go along with his conditions. "Lead on." He huffed as he ducked under the ivy and into a sloping tunnel.

Rufous took the lead, lighting the way with his trusty oil lamp. The sloping path was treacherous, made even more so by the near-constant rain that had lashed the town of late, though Rufous had no trouble whatsoever in navigating it. Percy, however, took three downward steps and slipped onto his sizeable rump with an undignified *splat*.

Rufous chuckled under his breath and carried on stalking ahead, leaving Percy to huff and curse as he examined the mud on the rear of his finely tailored trousers. Soon the tunnel levelled out and Percy caught up with his guide. "How much further?" he hissed.

"Not far now, sir," Rufous muttered. "We will be joining up with the old church catacombs in about a hundred yards."

The word *catacombs* made him shudder involuntarily. Rufous had never mentioned catacombs. He had been trying not to think about all the bones that lay above his head, but that single word made the image disturbingly vivid.

"They have a home of sorts in the catacombs," Rufous explained. "Though I can't say that it has many home comforts. Still, it keeps 'em off yer land, don't it?" A smirk creased his face. It felt good to get some solid digs in at his new employer while there was no fear of reprisals.

Percy grunted, "Let's get this over with"—and quickened the pace. He couldn't wait to sign the contract and open the floodgates for his inevitable wealth.

Eventually, the tunnel merged almost seamlessly with the stone walls of the ancient catacombs. Piles of bones littered the corners while the flagstones were covered in a carpet of dust and powder from pulverised remains. Rufous waded through the debris without so much as a flinch, while Percy tried his damnedest to avoid contact with even the smallest fragment of bone. Rufous grinned internally—he looked like an inept ballerina that was way past her prime.

"Halt!" a voice barked from the shadows. The word

was barely recognisable but had the desired effect. Percy let out a startled yelp and cowered behind Rufous.

"It's me, Rufous. We are here to see the boss man…as planned."

Scuffling movements in the impenetrable shadows announced that they had been surrounded. Percy could feel hundreds of furtive eyes roaming all over his body—no doubt admiring how much tender meat he had on his bones.

"Contract!" a particularly wizened creature barked as he stepped into the dim light afforded by the lamp. Its body was lean and hunched, with powerful hind legs and savage teeth in its dog-like muzzle. Its eyes glimmered with animal cunning as it sized Percy up and down.

"It's right here," Percy said in a tremulous voice as he removed a rolled document out of his pocket.

The elder ghoul looked at the paper, then glared directly into Percy's eyes. "Read!" he demanded with a jab of a sharply clawed finger.

Percy proceeded to read the document verbatim, but the overload of legal jargon made the elder snarl. Every time Percy said "whereupon," the ghoul got one step closer to ripping his throat out there and then.

Finally, dispensing with the prattle, Percy outlined the terms of the contract. The ghouls would clear the graves and *dispose* of the evicted cadavers as he instructed. In return, they would be guaranteed a supply of meat. This cut out any overheads Percy may have had, and the ghouls got fed. Everyone's a winner…except the families of the dearly departed, that is.

Percy signed with a flourish. The ghoul signed with a shaky X. The deal was struck and soon the money would be flooding in. Nothing could go wrong…right?

In the weeks that followed, the money did indeed come rolling in. Percy had his draughtsman draw up numerous bills, summonses, and seizure orders then got to work with his little red stamps. Every time he slammed ink down on the paper reading "paid," he could almost hear the money jingling in his coffers. Every time it said "seized," he could hear the munch of fang on flesh… He tried not to dwell too much on the second one.

The public was up in arms, as was to be expected. But there was little that anyone could do. He *was* the local government. He received so many death threats that he could have laid them end to end from his doorstep to London. Percy never batted an eyelid. And why would he? He had a gang of thugs on his payroll, who also did his debt collecting, and there was also the ghouls.

The denizens of the graveyard were more than happy with the deal. For the first time in so very long, they had more meat than they knew what to do with. This didn't mean for one second that the elder took his beady eyes off Percy. The scoundrel's middle name should have been duplicity.

How Percy ever dreamed that he could get away with such a despicable scheme for an extended period is a complete mystery. The man should have taken his money and run, but his rampant greed got the better of him as he sat and attempted to squeeze the very last ha'penny out of the town. Inevitably, the good times soon came to a crashing halt.

Percy had spent an enjoyable morning stamping documents and tallying up the day's take when he received a knock on his study door. When Percy opened it, he was surprised to be met by Rufous and a representative of Her Majesty Queen Victoria.

The austere-looking gentleman thrust a document, from the queen herself, into Percy's hand. The blood drained from his cheeks as he read. The queen wasn't amused…not in the slightest. Rufous smirked to himself, then slipped away like a shadow, while his employer was occupied.

Percy's legs buckled, and he flopped into his chair.

His jaw chattered, and sweat poured from his forehead. Not only had the queen stripped him of his job, title, and properties, along with overturning his *reprehensible* bill, she had also ordered that he pay back every single farthing that he had taken from the grief-stricken of Betyls Cove.

He should have anticipated that a ruler who was still mourning her beloved Albert would have taken a very dim view of such a scheme. He had one week to settle his accounts, pack up his belongings, and get out of town or a lengthy stay in one of her finest penal institutions would be his immediate fate.

Percy drank himself into oblivion as he wrote the cheques and distributed his wealth. For three days, he sat in a state of shock with the image of every pound and shilling dancing out of his bank vault with a jaunty step and a large grin. It was a marvel he didn't dehydrate due to the gallons of tears he shed.

It was late on the fourth evening when things got even worse for the former Sir Percy. It all began with a distinctive scrabbling from under the dining room floor. He was in the process of eating the contents of his larder, as he didn't want anyone else to get it after he was gone when he first noticed it. It sounded like a sizeable family of rats was tunnelling up into his home.

As a testament to how drunk he was, it took much

longer than it should for him to realise that if it was indeed rats…then they were as big as donkeys.

Percy screamed and fell backwards off his chair as the floorboards exploded in a shower of splinters. He held his soup spoon out in front of his chest in defence as the room was invaded by flesh-hungry ghouls.

"You can't be in here!" He tried to sound commanding, but the words shrank in his gullet. "We have a contract!"

The elder ghoul pushed his way to the front of the throng; he was flanked by Rufous Edwards. The gamekeeper grinned and held out the dirt-soiled contract. "It says here that my clients here…" He gestured around him.

"Your clients?" Percy exploded. "What the hell do you think you are playing at, man?"

Rufous cleared his throat and continued. "They are *guaranteed* by you to be paid in flesh."

"B-But…the deal's off. I've been removed from office. It's null and void, I'm afraid." A hint of his former cockiness returned to his tone.

"It says nothin' 'ere about the contract being torn up if you get removed or replaced." The ghouls growled hungrily as Rufous shook his head mockingly.

"Well, no…" Percy admitted. "But I never thought I

would be replaced! It's an outrage!"

"Well…" Rufous tutted. "The way we sees it is that *you* are in breach of contract and owe my clients a debt…"

"No…you don't mean?" Percy gabbled in terror.

"Bet you wish you'd just let me 'ave that rabbit now, don't yer?" Rufous chuckled and turned to the elder as he tore the contract in two. "I reckon it's about time you boys collected what's owed… Enjoy."

With one final chuckle, Rufous strode out of the room as the pack descended on Percy, ripping and tearing.

Rufous stood on the doorstep, placed one of Percy's cigars in his mouth, and sparked a Lucifer. As he breathed in the sweet smoke, Rufous thought to himself that it was nice to see someone who had taken so much, finally give something back to the town…

Dashboard Visitor

by K.B. Elijah

The red beast roared as it darted through the city, smoke oozing from its orifices. My hands were on the wheel, my feet on its pedals, and it growled in response.

"Did you see his face as it happened?" Heather snickered from the passenger seat of the second-hand car, slapping the dashboard with a gloved hand. Her voice was raspy, cracked with the weight of a thousand cigarettes, and the cloying smell clung to her even on the rare occasions that she didn't have one pressed between her thin lips. Now was one of those times, the ecstatic thrill of what we were doing enough to temporarily sustain her through even a nicotine craving, although I noticed that that the fingers on her right hand twitched every so often as if plucking an imaginary cigarette from her mouth.

"See who?" I asked, turning my gaze back to the road ahead. It was quiet at this time of night, and although that was good for speed, it was bad for attracting attention. I'd needed to cut through the industrial district to put as much space as I could between us and the bank as quickly as possible, but now I angled west towards the residential areas, hoping to mingle among the bleary-eyed traffic of early risers and shift workers.

I felt, rather than saw, the disdainful look Heather shot my way.

"Not you," she snapped. "You were out in the car, warming your ass while we did the real work."

I bit my tongue to keep it from the bitter retort I knew I'd later regret. It may seem like the easy job when viewed from the outside, sitting around while my colleagues pulled off the actual heist, but it was like comparing improv to real acting. Sure, they spent a heated five minutes disabling alarms and cutting through doors, but that was *it*. I'd dedicated the last five weeks of my life to plotting routes, canvassing neighbourhoods, arranging back-up vehicles and drop-off points… even the ass-warming took skill. It wasn't like I could just pull up in front of the building and play some tunes while I waited, like they do in the movies. It was about picking a park that was close enough to the exit to collect everyone with the most efficient timing, having line of sight but not being in the direct view of any cameras or passers-by, not breaching any road regulations or catching anyone's attention…

"Nah, man, she's talking about this wimpy-ass night guard we found," Carlo said from the seat behind me, his lazy drawl as frustrating as ever. "Dude made the epic mistake of getting in our way."

My eyes flicked to his in the rear-view mirror. He was already watching me, as if anticipating my reaction.

"Night guard?" I asked, alarmed. "I thought we'd dealt with that already by paying our guy off?"

Carlo shrugged. "Guess this newbie didn't get the message to take the night off. But we certainly *dealt with* him."

Heather let out a guffaw, a braying laugh that drowned out the chuckles of the two men in the back seat.

"What the fuck did you do?" I yelled, my attention wavering from the road for a moment and returning just in time to avoid veering onto the path.

The atmosphere in the car turned chilly, despite the seat warmers that I did indeed have heating our asses. Everyone but Heather's: hers was conveniently broken. The perils of second-hand cars, and all that.

"Derek, you fucking wuss," Heather snapped, slapping my forearm. "You think we were going to forfeit *six million* for one wannabe cop?"

"I think," I said coldly, "that if you killed someone, we're going to have a serious problem."

"Oh really?" Carlo asked, his voice far too close to my ear, and I stiffened as I felt the cold steel of his knife at my throat. Resting his chin on the top of my seat, he pressed his cheek to my own. My head swam and my foot pressed down further on the accelerator, ready to drive straight at a fucking wall if that's what it took for him to unhand me. "Do we have a problem, Little D?"

I felt Carlo jerk as Raj nudged him with his foot. "Chill, dude," he said, and from the relaxed tone of voice, it sounded like he was taking his own advice. "What's done is done. Derek was just worrying about our safety, weren't you?"

I looked at Raj in the mirror, his soft brown eyes boring into mine with humour…and also warning.

"Yeah," I muttered, and the pressure on my neck eased as Carlo stopped humping the back of my seat and leaned back into his own.

"Besides," Raj continued, slapping the duffel resting between him and Carlo. It gave a satisfying chink, the telltale sound of heavy gold bars clipping together. "It was all worth it. That guard would have dobbed us in if we'd let him walk out of there, you see? We had to take care of him, for the greater good and all that." He shrugged, catching my eye again. "One of him, and four of us? Even more when we consider what we're going to use this money for. Think of your girl, Little D. You can give her everything she deserves—get her out of that shithole and away from her old man. You're *saving her life*."

I sighed, nodding. It was true. That bastard of a man Leisa called her father would ruin her if I didn't get her out of there soon, but she'd only do it if we had "stability." I was going to give her fucking stability. All $1.5 mil of it.

"He knew the risks." Heather sniffed, tossing her short hair over her shoulder. The moment she moved her head again, the dirty blonde strands reverted to their original position. "Could have worked at Maccas, but no, the guy had to be a hero. And a hero is what he'll be when they find him, I'm sure."

"Here," Raj said softly and leaned forward to drop something heavy into my lap. I initially flinched, relaxing when I realised what it was.

The golden glow of the bar, glinting in the flickering streetlights as we raced through the city, felt like it was giving off actual warmth, despite the fact that I could feel its chill through my jeans. I took a hand from the steering wheel to touch it, my fingers caressing the outlines of the gold like it was Leisa's hips. This was real. That random night guard without a name was not. I wasn't there; it wasn't my fault. What the hell could I have done about it? But this—*this* was what mattered. I could make myself. Forge a name, a life, a family. I needed it more than I'd ever needed anything before, the urge pressing into me like a physical weight in my chest matching the heft of the gold on my lap.

Heather's eyes bore into my crotch with undisguised longing.

"Like something you see?" I asked, in a lame attempt to diffuse the tension, pausing at a stop sign at a deserted intersection. The time for going fast was over; now it was about obeying road rules to avoid drawing attention.

Heather snorted, but my words brought a different kind of attention, the unwanted type.

"I do," Carlo drawled, reaching a hand forward to trail it lightly down my neck. The guy was inexplicably hot and cold. One minute with a knife to my neck, the next his goddamn fingers? I shrugged him off.

"You're wasting your breath. Derek's straighter than a…telegraph pole," Heather said, trailing off when she couldn't think of a better analogy.

"Those fuckers aren't straight." Carlo laughed. "Or are you trying to tell me something?"

"A ruler," I volunteered, ignoring Carlo. "A ruler's straight."

I knew I'd made a mistake when I saw his eyes glitter in the rear-view mirror. "A ruler is—"

Whatever disgusting insinuation he was about to

make was cut off by Raj.

"Guys," he said loudly. "We are now six million dollars richer. For the love of gold, Little D, give us some music!"

Bolstered by the gold in my grasp, I obligingly put my hand to the radio as everyone cheered. My fingers fumbled on the unfamiliar layout, and I pulled my eyes from the road for a moment to find the volume dial.

"Fuck!" I yelled, wrenching the steering wheel as an honest-to-god miniature person appeared on the dashboard above the radio. "What the hell is that?"

Chaos erupted, with Carlo yelping and Raj shouting and Heather attempting to shoo the thing away by waving her arms and accidentally cuffing me on the jaw.

I fought to get the car back under control, my breathing frantic as I battled the internal war of wanting to stop and run from the car as if a spider had just crawled into my pants, and simultaneously wanting to drive faster as if it was a bug on the windshield I could blow off in the wind.

But the creature was neither a spider nor a bug.

It was a *she*, I realised, as I took a second, more cautious look at the dashboard. She perched atop the dusty plastic, as steady and unwavering as if her feet had been glued to the surface, and while the rest of us thrashed and yelled, she stood serenely in an image of patience, her pale blue dress flickering in an unfelt wind.

It was only when we'd finally calmed down, and Heather had stopped trying to squish her with the tattered shoe she'd slipped from her foot—ineffectively, as the shoe passed through the woman and slapped the dashboard as if she wasn't there at all—that the miniature person spoke.

"You have something of mine," she said, her tiny mouth moving in a lifelike way. Her voice was musical, melodious even, and it suited the petite figure in a way I couldn't quite describe. Fairy-like.

"Fuck off," Heather growled, brandishing her shoe in a way that was supposed to be threatening, but considering that it couldn't do a thing to the woman, just looked stupid. "We have nothing of anyone's."

The woman's eyes flickered past her, and I realised she was looking at the duffel bag. I heard the sound of colliding gold again and assumed either Raj or Carlo had scooped it up protectively.

"Wrong," the woman said icily. "That is *mine*."

She lifted her chin. "Do you fools need an introduction? I am Evangeline Carmody, lady of the city."

Raj and I gasped in unison.

"Who the hell is that?" Carlo asked dully, and I

growled at his stupidity.

"The owner of the bank we just robbed, you *moron*."

"Oh" was all he said. "Well, tell her to fuck off."

"I already did, remember?" Heather said. "She ignored me, which was downright rude."

"Forget ignoring," Raj said, and his usually amused voice was tight and terse. "It's worse than that."

"Worse than the owner of the bank somehow tracking us down?" Heather asked, her own voice unusually high pitched. "She's probably got the police on our tail! I hate magic!"

I shook my head. "I put anti-law enforcement tracking spells on us before the heist." Because that was what I do, you dismissive and haughty cow.

"Worse," Raj confirmed. "Lady Carmody is a leprechaun."

That explained how she'd done the whole "appearing in the car" thing. It was just a projection: leprechauns were good at illusions, and it meant that she was probably quite normal-sized in her true form. The ache in my chest grew, and suddenly I wanted quite badly to meet her in person, to draw those beautifully shaped lips to mine, to fist my hands in that golden hair and make her—

Lady Carmody let out a thin smile. "Well done, *troll*," she said dismissively, and Raj growled, his tusks snapping at her.

We all bristled at the disgusted way she shaped the word. We might not be the prettiest species, but we didn't deserve the stereotypical disdain perpetually doled out to us: had we not just proved ourselves clever enough to trick a leprechaun from her gold?

"I will not bring the police on you," she added, spreading her arms as if we should be astounded by her generosity. Although to be fair, I was.

Heather poked a finger in her direction. "If you're expecting something in return, forget it," she hissed. "The gold is ours."

"Of course," Lady Carmody said agreeably. "Of course, it must be. I hereby gift the full value of it to you, lovely people."

Raj let out a despairing howl and threw himself forward, his hands clawing ineffectively at the dashboard mirage.

"Get a hold of yourself," Heather snapped, wrenching him backwards from where he had practically fallen in her lap. I turned another corner, grateful to see the warm glow of houses ahead. We had made it to the residential districts, and there were no sirens within earshot. Were we free?

"The gold," Raj moaned. "The gold!"

Something didn't feel right. I glanced down to find the gold bar, whose weight had been so comfortable and reassuring, now gone. Had it slipped from my lap while I wasn't watching? Had Raj taken it back? Had—

"What the fuck?" Carlo screeched, waving the duffel bag in the rear-view mirror. The fabric sagged limply, clearly empty. My heart stopped at the sight. "Where has it gone?"

Lady Carmody pressed her hands together as if in mock prayer. "A leprechaun's gold is merely an illusion, my dearest trolls. You should have done your research on that before robbing me, although clearly *one* of you knew." She directed her gaze to Raj, who seethed quietly in the back seat. "It seems he had not intended on sharing that with the rest of you: perhaps he was intending to exchange his share for something of real value before the night was out?"

I braked hard, not bothering to put on the handbrake as I twisted in my seat. "You—"

But my words were drowned out by the accusations of Heather and Carlo as they also rounded on Raj with desperate and pissed off accusations.

"How could you—"

"All that work—"

"It's fucking gone!"

"What do we do *now*?"

"I need that money—"

"You'll pay for this!"

As we bickered and squabbled, and Carlo pulled out his knife with a wicked glint in his eye, Lady Carmody watched from her perch on the filthy dashboard with something like satisfaction on her face.

"Normally," she said, "that would be the end of the tale. Karmic gratification by way of the loss of any reward. But in this case, you did something much, *much* worse than steal an illusion."

Her eyes flashed dangerously. "You killed an innocent man, you disgusting cowards," she spat, the musical quality of her voice now absent. "You'll suffer in return for the blind depravity of your greed."

"And what are you going to do about it, fairy lady?" Heather taunted, pulling a face at her. "Illusion some ghosts to haunt us?"

I swallowed. That sounded pretty terrifying.

But Heather seemed unfazed, pulling a cigarette from her coat pocket and poking it between her lips as Raj let out a pained squeal, underpinned by Carlo's deep and unrestrained laughter. I didn't look around, and I kept my eyes firmly away from the rear-view mirror, even as the squelch of wet flesh met my ears.

"*I'm* not going to do anything," Lady Carmody said with a twist of her lips. "But the brother of the deceased has his own intentions." She glanced at the unlit cigarette dangling from Heather's yellowed teeth, her eyes flickering with amusement. "Need a light for that?"

The dashboard visitor flickered out of existence as I caught movement out of the corner of my eye: a huge red plume of fire erupting from the mouth of a monstrous scarlet dragon planted in the street ahead of us. Goddamn distracting leprechaun.

I looked down at my lap, wishing I could hold the gold bar one last time, feel its smooth skin against my own.

I wanted more. I needed more. I *deserved* more.

The dragon gazed with smouldering eyes at the blazing wreck at its feet, the writhing figures of blackened char letting out pathetic little mewling noises. It grimaced, far from content, but a small portion of its grief burned away with the bodies of the thieving, murderous trolls.

Howling, it took off into the air, its great wings fanning the flames of the vehicle. The red beast roared as it darted through the city, smoke oozing from its orifices.

Apsaras' Dance

by Kelly Matsuura

Time wastes the paint on our faces and ornaments. It roughens the once-smooth stone we were carved from. Yet behind the crumbling stone, we shine.

Our voices blend as we step from the wall, magic infusing our limbs and lighting our smiles. We sing the songs of ancient apsaras before us.

Once, we were a single goddess in the Heavens. Now, we are a thousand faces with a collective soul on Earth. We were awakened one by one, charmed by the moon to dance freely under Vishnu's stars.

We honour the gods of Mount Meru from the vacated palace of Angkor Wat. Once a king's home and now his living legacy.

We dance each night with pure abandon—eyes closed, our faces tilted to the sky. Each one of us unique, each voice a varied note merging in harmony.

One night, we step out from the walls and take our usual positions. But something is different. Someone watches from the shadows of the ruins. A man, sitting alone on a blanket. He presses a flute to his lips and plays a delicate tune. Slow at first, then growing in tempo and volume as we quicken our dance.

We enjoy this new music. It's invigorating, tickling our toes as we step to the rhythm. We move through the ruins, twirling our skirts and waving our hands. Vishnu smiles down and offers his applause.

The man ends his tune and packs his belongings away. He then does a most surprising thing—he moves to the nearest apsara and wraps his arms around her waist from behind. His hands glow and send a pulse of blue light through the apsara's transparent form. She fills out into a solid figure and looks around in confusion. The man then pulls her with him as he runs off into the jungle.

Has he made her human? He must realise that she has no soul of her own. It is a most curious event.

We do not see the strange man nor his stolen bride for many months. When he returns, he is alone and plays his flute once again. He plays the same tune as before, and after playing, he captures another apsara. We watch him go with less curiosity than before.

Two months later, he returns for another. Then he comes monthly for a while, during the full moon. More apsaras disappear with him into the jungle.

We continue our nightly moon dance, still numbering over nine hundred. We space ourselves a little further apart in the grounds.

Now, he comes weekly. He plays a new song. Faster, frantic. We twirl and sparkle just for him, enchanted by the skill of his lips and fingers on that magic flute. He becomes our god on those nights.

Vishnu does not stay to watch this grand performance. He devotes his time to other temple maids, in other lands, other cities.

We should mind, but no, we are adored by the flutist. We blush at the sight of him and bow as he takes a new bride from our troop.

As he runs into the jungle with apsara number 204 by his side, we feel a deep loneliness. We wish for more music, to dance longer, to feel loved. We ache until the next week, when our god returns.

The rainy season begins. Not our favourite time of year, but still we dance for the moon. The flutist comes weekly still too, but now he takes two apsaras each visit.

They make a charming sight: a man holding hands with two beautiful dancers in the rain. They skip through the temple grounds along the trail to the jungle, their bracelets jingling, their wet saris sticking to their skin, and their bare feet kicking up mud.

We wave goodbye to our lucky sisters. Surely, they will have a blessed life.

When they have gone, we release our tears. For we are still here, locked in the ruined walls and silent daytime of this place.

Vishnu looks down upon this scene, two arms folded across his chest, a frown on his imposing face. He does not speak a word, nor ask us to dance. He turns his back, and the sky darkens.

Another night. The man returns but does not sit in his usual place. He places his blanket near the east corner, facing Garuda, the chosen vehicle of Vishnu. For as long as we have existed in this place, Garuda has remained an attentive but silent patron to our performance.

All our lost sisters accompany the man. They kneel in rows behind him, bowing to their master.

The man draws his flute to his lips, then pauses. We, locked in the wall, hold our breath. We cannot step out without music now. He has taken too many of us, and our power is now weak.

Instead of the regular song, the flutist plays a dark, awakening melody. We are slow to recognise it, not having heard the piece for centuries, but when we do, we fear for our own existence.

He plays the ancient composition, created by the Dark Ones. Just as our song releases us from the stone walls, this piece will release Garuda from his entombment. No more will he be confined to his sentry duties.

The music grows and peaks. It drains magic from the temple stones, our very soul, and the great moon above. Where is our lord to protect us?

Our numbers are small—we have not attracted Vishnu's interest for some time. He is nowhere to be seen.

The statue of Garuda begins to ripple on the surface. Light glows from deep within. Garuda awakes; he is ready for his long-awaited freedom. The flutist steps closer, still playing the dark notes of the spell.

Light emerges from the stone and takes shape. Garuda stands tall, raises his head, and spreads his giant wings. He is both light and darkness in equal balance.

The man draws out the last note, lowering the flute and keeping his gaze steady on Garuda. He kneels and bows his head in honour.

Garuda roars, coming to life. But the song is not enough to give him physical form. He is far larger than us apsaras and has a greater need for power to exist in the human world. Without a solid form, he will return to stone.

The young man had well prepared. He rises to his feet and takes two steps towards Garuda. He holds his hands out in front of him, and they glow with the blue light we have seen before. But this time, it is beyond beautiful. It is exquisite in both shade and brightness, like the rarest of blue diamonds.

He joins hands with Garuda. The blue energy passes between them, blinding in its expansion and speed. When it fades and we can see again, Garuda is gone.

The man now holds Garuda within and can shift between forms at will.

He changes now in mere seconds. Man becomes beast. Garuda gives a final roar of farewell. He takes to the sky, not looking back, for he surely knows our sorrow can never be undone.

We are the apsaras of Angkor Wat. Remember us. Remember our love of dance and spare a tear for us.

Greed

The Avarice of Death

by Lyndsey Ellis-Holloway

"Thanatos!"

Sammael stopped in his tracks, eyebrows furrowed at the use of his Grecian name in the Golden City. No one in Heaven referred to him as such, only his beloved, Atropos. She wasn't supposed to be here.

Why did she sound so panicked? He'd never heard that tone from his wife before, not in all the centuries he'd known her. Always calm and collected, nothing fazed her—not the disgust the Heavens felt toward their union, nor the further hatred faced at birthing a Nephilim. What could possibly have brought his wife to Heaven?

Glancing around, he ushered Atropos off the main street. He used his golden wings to shield her from view as they made their way out past the ornate Golden Gates, following the path to Eden.

"Ati? What's wrong?" he asked once they were deep into the garden, surrounded by the myriad of plants found in every region of the world below them. Sammael opened his arms to the slight woman as she threw herself into him. Her body collided with his, his armour singing as the metal of her wedding band struck his backplate with the force of her embrace. "Ati, why are you here? You know better than to come here, Father and the others don't approve. We're *so* close!" he whispered, his tone harsh.

"It's Alina. She's been taken," she whispered, her voice trembling as she turned her face toward him. The colour had drained from her cheeks, her usually calm grey eyes now wide and full of fear.

Any further reprimand was pushed aside as a lump formed in his throat, his body numb and shaking as he tried to swallow his rage. Alina—his Little Light. When God assigned Sammael his task, the Archangel had gone about his duties without question; throwing mind, body, and soul into his work. Until he met Atropos.

Sammael had never encountered a more beautiful, and electrifying, woman than the third sister of the Grecian Fates known as the Moirai. While he worked closely with her sisters, Clotho and Lachesis, it was Atropos who cut the threads of life for the Greeks, therefore it was Ati he spent the majority of his time with.

It was subtle at first, flirtation was not natural to Sammael. Her body brushing against his as she reached for her scissors, her fingertips lingering on his as she asked him to hold the thread while she cut it. Suddenly he was spending more and more time with her—taking her to the Elysian Fields, sneaking her into Eden to ask her to be his wife, conceiving Alina in the Hanging Gardens of Babylon.

From the moment of her birth, she became his everything, his light, and she had accelerated his and Atropos' plans. Working with the Moirai had led to finding a kindred spirit, it took very little to persuade Atropos and her sisters to aid Sammael in his plan to grow in power. He wanted to knock that insufferable Gabriel from his spot as God's Right Hand, to make his older brother suffer for what Gabriel had done to Sammael's twin sister. With the Moirai by his side, Sammael would achieve that.

In the beginning that had been as far as his ambitions stretched—to gain more power, push his brother from his pedestal, gaining the recognition and strength that Sammael strived to have—the birth of his daughter fuelled that fire. He wanted to eliminate the distractions from his life, whittling out the lesser gods from the other religions whom he currently had to visit for their lists.

It took all of Sammael's strength not to buckle under the weight of her words. Her tone struck his heart cold, as though she'd pierced it with a knife—soon that fear dissipated, replaced by the rising tide of rage at the insolence that anyone would dare take his child.

"Ati, who has her?" he asked, his voice low, full of such menace that his wife looked up in shock and stepped back. Her eyes grew wide as she met the piercing blue gaze of her husband, the iris ringed with the molten gold halo of the Angels.

"Namtar, he left a note for you on Alina's bed, He says if we want her back we have to go to the Gardens and meet his demands."

"Demands? *Demands*?! Does that lesser god think he can make *demands* of *me*?! He will regret touching our daughter. Come Ati," Sammael snarled, taking her hand in his, striding out of Eden, the tips of his feathers shedding embers with each footfall.

It had been some time since Sammael frequented the Hanging Gardens of Babylon. Decades ago he and Atropos spent hours in the beauty of this place, surrounded by the most vibrant flowers, the gentle breeze carrying the sweetest scents. They'd enjoyed one another's company beneath the swaying willows, listening to the trickling fountains, secretly plotting how to get what they wanted from their lives. The first time they'd admitted wanting more than their current stations allowed had been here, in fact, that had been the day they'd conceived Alina, at the very top of the Gardens amongst the roses.

When Alina had been little Sammael and Atropos brought their daughter here to play as often as time allowed. He adored watching his Little Light waddle across the paved walkways, hands held towards the sky, her fingers curling and uncurling as she chased after butterflies and bees, giggling all the while.

It had been here that he'd taught Alina how to summon forth her wings, as a Nephilim the task took a little more thought than that of a full-blooded Angel, and showed her how to fly. He remembered standing at the top of the waterfall at the southern end of the Gardens, her hand in his, Alina grinning excitedly as she leapt into the air with her father, flying high above the Gardens to the enthusiastic applause of her mother below.

Now Sammael saw none of that beauty, his eyes narrowed as he and Atropos sought the enemy who had taken their beloved child from them.

"Namtar! Show yourself!" Sammael demanded, his voice booming through the entirety of the Gardens, shaking their very foundations. "You had best not anger me further, the audacity of your actions may yet be forgiven if you return Alina immediately. Do not think to test my patience on this matter."

"The audacity of *my* actions? What about your own,

Nergal? Do not think me naïve, I know what you and the Moirai are up to—you seek to cut me out entirely, to take my position from me and the others like me, so that only her and her sisters are left to serve you in the realms of Death."

"What nonsense do you spout Namtar?" Sammael growled, it had been so long since he'd visited the lesser God of Fate that he'd almost forgotten his Mesopotamian name until Namtar spoke it. He'd intended on killing the lesser god, along with all the others tied to his duties, in order to leave only the Moirai at his disposal—now he regretted not taking action sooner, now Alina suffered because Sammael'd been too kind.

His eyes searched the pathways as he and Atropos made their way through the Gardens, heading for the centre where he assumed the fool was hidden—it was the bottom tier of the Gardens, the way Namtar's voice carried on the wind came from below where Sammael and Atropos arrived. Slipping an arm around Atropos' waist Sammael stepped off the edge of the Garden, flying them down with ease.

"Does your avarice have no end that you do not realise what you are doing to the rest of us?" Namtar's voice was louder now. "You took my job from me, you stopped coming to me for the count. I work tirelessly for you in your posting, just as Atropos and her sisters do, just as *all* the others in positions such as mine have always done. Yet you stopped coming to me, in favour of *her*. She's stepped beyond her remit, I know she's been measuring the strands for Mesopotamia as well as Greece. That is *my* position and you seek to take it. I will not stand idly by while you push me aside Nergal, I will not be a stepping stone for you seeking to take the crown in Heaven!"

How had the lesser god worked out their plans? With only the Moirai to deal with, he could anticipate his Father's requests *ahead* of time not to mention he could spend more time with his wife and daughter. Taking the lists from the Moirai, he could do his duty and return to his girls in good time. Or so had been the plan.

Sammael growled under his breath, hands balled into fists, the flames in his wings no longer smouldering at the ends but flickering across each feather, a living thing. As he reached the centre, he spotted Namtar atop one of the Gardens' many statues—the Mesopotamian was hard to miss, his dark skin a stark contrast to the white and gold robes he wore, his black beard full and well trimmed in the the typically Arabic style of his people. Namtar held Alina's trembling form held against his body, hand tight around her throat. She looked to be no more than fourteen, the spitting image of her mother with her slight frame and braided golden hair—but she had his eyes, pools of clear blue with the faintest shimmer of a golden ring.

"Release my daughter Namtar, I will not ask you again," Sammael said darkly, his gaze flickering to his daughter who could not speak because of Namtar's hold on her neck, but the look in her eyes was enough to make his heart break. "It's alright Little Light, daddy's here now," he added softly.

"Not until you swear you will give my duties back to me! I will not be forgotten Nergal. I will not be pushed out by your Grecian wench and your need to be all-powerful!" Namtar's thick, dark eyebrows furrowed

"You forget yourself Namtar." Sammael reprimanded.

"*No*! You forget *yourself* Nergal, You want the power of your position *and* this little family of yours, but in the pursuit of that, you have cast the rest of us aside. I will not allow your desire to consume you in this fashion, I will not be a casualty of your avarice!" Namtar screamed. The lesser god visibly trembled as his grip tightened instinctively on Alina's throat, her dainty fingers clawing at his hands as her mouth opened and closed, gasping for air until there was an audible 'snap'.

Time stood still as silence filled the Gardens.

Atropos' scream shattered it. Namtar eyes threatened to pop from their sockets as Sammael's burning glare flickered from the limp form of his daughter to the lesser god. Namtar flinched, letting go of Alina and allowing her to fall from the statue into the waiting arms of her mother. Atropos wailed as she held her daughter in her arms, rocking back and forth.

His wife's keen was drowned out by the deafening beat of his heart as Sammael lowered his head slightly, eyes never leaving Namtar's frozen frame.

"N-Nergal… I didn't mean to—I'm sorry," Namtar whimpered, flinching under the dark gaze of the Angel of Death.

In a heartbeat, Sammael crossed the courtyard, grabbing Namtar by the throat, fingernails digging into the lesser god's throat, drawing blood. Sammael relished in the snap of skin and sinew, crushing the gasping Namtar's windpipe. "I told you not to test me," Sammael snapped, Namtar's bulging eyes rolling back in his purple, swelling face just as the Archangel released his throat.

Namtar drew in a breath, collapsing upon his knees at Sammael's feet, gasping and spluttering, head bowed to the man he should never have challenged, Sammael put a hand to his hip. The air crackled with electricity, the smell of hot metal heavy as the air beneath his hand wavered, sword and scabbard appearing from nothing. his Scythe.

Sammael's fingers wrapped around the sword's hilt, the metal sang as he drew it—the broadsword shimmering as it changed into a scimitar as was appropriate for his position as Nergal.

Namtar looked up, but the lesser god never had the chance to realise, nor fear, what was about to happen—two hands upon Scythe's hilt Sammael let loose a cry, slicing Namtar's head from his neck cleanly. Flicking Scythe in his hands, he slammed the tip between the lesser god's eyes, cleaving the impudent fool's head in two. He stared at the lifeless eyes, the barest flicker of satisfaction running through him—one step towards his goals completed. But at what cost? What good was power now that his reason for being had been taken from him? What had his greed got him?!

Sammael kicked Namtar's body away as he turned towards Atropos' wails—the sound of her mourning hitting him as though the Heavens themselves had fallen from the sky. Each unsteady step he took toward his wife and daughter felt like he was wading through mud, Sammael could not tear his eyes away from his daughter, cradled in her weeping mother's arms.

This wasn't happening, this was all a lie, she would

be fine, of course she would, she was *his* daughter. She was merely asleep, unconscious from the stress and pain she had suffered—how could she be dead? She was the daughter of the Angel of Death.

He couldn't bring her back, that wasn't in his remit, God had not been foolish enough to allow Death to give life *back*. Some deaths Sammael had no control over. While *most* deaths were pre-arranged, the deaths of beings like himself, Namtar and Alina were harder to predict, in fact only God *truly* knew… if He knew at all.

Sammael collapsed beside Atropos, dragging Alina from her into his own embrace, cradling his daughter against his chest as he breathed slowly and deeply, his body trembling. Sammael's grip on his daughter tightened, his eyes and hair began to glow with a blinding golden light, forcing Atropos to cover her eyes and look away. The grief was too much to bear, the weight of it heavy on Sammael's heart as his feathers roared to life, flames trickled down his back and shoulders, his emotions began consuming him.

"Wait, Thanatos, she's breathing. Thanatos, Alina's breathing!" Atropos called beside him, Sammael barely registered her voice, all sense of reason lost now. "Thanatos stop! Listen to me! She's alive, our daughter's alive, she's *breathing*!" she continued, voice cracking as she reached to take Alina from him, swiftly withdrawing her hand—burnt by the flames. "Thanatos! *Sammael please!*"

Atropos cries were consumed in the roaring blaze that enveloped her husband, their daughter in his arms, forcing Atropos to run from her family lest she too be caught in the fire. Sammael could not register anything but the loss of his daughter, everything they'd been working for had been for Alina. He'd failed her; she'd been hurt by his actions, because of *his* ambitions.

Unable to control himself or the fire within, Sammael bellowed. Alina looked up at him, mouthing the word '*daddy*'. She was alive? He fought desperately to regain control of his flames, but it was too late. With an audible 'boom', the fire burst from his body like a nuclear explosion—destroying everything in its path.

As suddenly as they had appeared the fires died. Sammael's hands trembled as he looked at the ash pooled there, the heat replaced with ice-cold reality. The searing pain in his chest left him breathless and for a moment he thought his mind would break alongside his heart.

What remained of his daughter was taken by the gentle breeze that whipped through the remnants of the Garden. The pillars that held the upper tiers collapsed around him, crumbling arches and statues followed suit as the breeze brushed them. Once beautiful flower beds and vibrant plant life were burnt beyond recognition, the fire had fed upon them, All that remained was ash and scorched earth.

Slowly he stood, cinders falling from his lap. Namtar's remains were charred, raw flesh blistered under the fierce intensity of Sammael's uncontrolled emotions. Scythe no longer by the head, having returned to its rightful place by Sammael's side.

It took all his strength to move his feet as he left the ruined Gardens, not daring to meet Atropos' horrified face as he abandoned his wife, and the life they'd built, in Babylon. This was his punishment; this was his doing just as Namtar had said. Icarus had flown too close to the Sun and burnt his wings, falling to his death—Sammael had *been* the Sun, only he'd reached too high and his daughter burned because of it.

*Father was right. I'm a soldier; created to follow **His** orders. This is my punishment for stepping out of line, for thinking I was strong enough to go against God. I'm the Angel of Death; Death is all I shall have, what a fool I've been for wanting more than what God allows.*

Sammael stopped, turning his face upwards, eyes closed as the breeze tenderly caressed his face—leaving behind traces of ash that stuck to the tears trailing down his cheeks. Brushing the tears from his face, Sammael smeared the char across his skin as he did so, spreading his wings, ready to return home.

His punishment wouldn't be over here, he had Father and Gabriel to face. The memory of Alina's fear and confusion as her father's flames tore her apart was enough to ensure he would not seek for things above his station *ever* again.

Pretty Little Twisting Ladders

by Hari Navarro

Passing headlights ignite the leaden twilight glow and it pierces, fingering through the window slats, undulating slices of sticky night cast across the sublime recline of her naked form. Living serpentine shadows segment the smoke that pulses between her fingers, creep on the ruined plain of her strewn sheets, and then rear up across the strap-on that glistens between my legs.

"Happy birthday," I coo from beneath the Venetian carnival mask that covers my face entirely.

"Thank you," she says picking a non-existent slither of tobacco from the very tip of her tongue and rolling it, flicking it onto the bed.

"No, you don't. You don't thank me. If anything, you thank yourself. You created this moment. You have the financial prowess to create any moment of your pleasing. This moment and I are just but one of the many."

"Interesting, not only does it climax like a straining cow but also it speaks. You are jealous, perhaps? You deny me this life I have built? Do you not have one, poor little thing? You know nothing. You do not know who I am. Fuck, you probably don't know who you are." She smiles, this time pinching and playing with the thick swell of her bottom lip as she shoots a gust of smoke and condescension between the clench of her perfectly whitened teeth.

"You are right, for the most part, at least. I really don't know who you are. So, tell me. Talk to me. I'm interested, really I am. Go on, tell me just who the fuck you are."

She twists, agitated, into the glow, and I notice again the grey threads that sit nestling amongst the black of her hair. Such a strange paradox, this woman. So vain, so sure of herself yet so surely lost. I think she is crying. There are no tears but I can hear the quiver from the very pit of her throat.

She swallows. She fixes her gaze.

"So fastidiously I pretended that I was a certain thing, for years I have played this part. If those around me had cared to look, they'd have well seen my ruse. My parents, my friends, my lovers, their jaws all moving in lock-step sync, like fucking marionettes. Trapdoors to nowhere that slide up and down. Up and down. My lie, it was most obvious..."

I'm sorry…I know she is in that middle of this big unasked for emotional reveal, but I can't stop staring at her breasts. They really are works of art. A grotesquely expensive artisan surgeon's masterwork, I am sure. I mean they look perfect and they feel perfectly real but there must be silicon in that valley within which I am sure many before me have found themselves so irreversibly and completely lost.

Sorry. Continue.

Fuck, she finished. Missed the ass end of that one. No mind, I'm sure she'll tell me again.

"But they didn't, did they, look that is? Well, they may well have looked but they surely did not see you, am I right? They had no idea of the person." I scramble to regain my footing, and my words sound forced and hollow, even to me.

Anyway. Moving on.

"You are playing me. You're telling me nothing more than exactly what I want to hear. You are just like the others. Just another in this queue that I must work my way through—you who smooth your eyes across my beautiful body, the priceless flesh that I have abused and moulded just so. I have travelled to the ends of the earth; I have fucked the greatest minds in science to try and sate the worm that curls foetal at the centre of my existence. I pretended to be good. To be more than content with my lot. But I wasn't. I always wanted…"

"…more. You wanted more. Right, more is all we ever really need."

"You can leave now. I know what you are up to. Many others have tried. You all fail. Such false empathy as you reach and glean and tongue from my husk."

"Why am I here, do you think? Is it sheer dumb luck that brought us together?"

"Christ, listen to yourself, you afford this night so much more than it deserves. It was a fuck. Consider yourself fucked."

"Aren't you tired? Tired of doing this—it must take its toll. All this posturing and judging."

"Maybe you are right. These masquerade parties are not for the likes of you. I was wrong, I thought through them I'd be able to find the answer. That's because I sealed you all in masks, all that would be left was the truth."

"Come now, you don't really want the truth, do you?"

"You fucking people, you maggots—you feast at my expense and you take what you want. But know, I give you nothing. Nothing. And know also that you are definitely not the one. You are a terrible fuck, plus your lips are too thin and your thighs are too fucking fat. Oh, and your tits are all wrong."

"You don't believe that. I am different, aren't I? And you, my dearest, know it full well. You singled me out, excised me from the baying, fawning mass. You saw me. You saw me and you knew. I am just like you."

"Don't make me fucking laugh, I tried you on. You are a garment, that is all. You are nothing like me. You all see the wet swell of my upturned lips and yet never once listen to a single fucking word that they say. You flounder in the gently agitating tidepools of my eyes and drown in the sheen that washes the perfect jut of my breasts, but you didn't see that I am filling right up to the brim. You didn't see as I tried to find myself. You didn't see the dirty stains that finger the side of the cup."

"But I did, I did see you. I think your road is but a ginnel, an alleyway to another road. I'm here to listen, to travel it with you. And fuck, but mostly, mostly to listen. Really, I could listen to your sanctimonious mournful swill day in and day fucking out. I'm here for you."

She is falling. She is putting on a brave face but it is as fake as the one that ties in a pretty red bow at the back of my head. She is starting to come apart. Poor thing. Listen, listen now as she makes no sense. Tying herself up and tripping, over and over again.

"You expect me to suck on the dirt that cakes your words, there're holes in my hands. I don't believe you, but can't you see that I couldn't hold on to you if I did? What do you want of me, what do you fucking well need?"

See what I mean. Nonsensical. Swill.

Sorry.

Anyway.

"I need and I want everything, all of you and more besides."

"Then, you will have nothing. I took all I could and I used it up for all it was worth, drained the fucker dry. I stripped my family bare of its wealth; I dug up and pried the gold from the teeth of my ancestors."

"Really?"

"No, I'm not a fucking animal. I'm just trying to paint a picture here."

"In the end, when we do our final tally, the things that we have left amount to everything. What is it that you are missing? What is it that you crave that your vast intellect and wealth cannot provide? What have you been looking for in all that have passed through your bed?"

"I was searching for something, wasn't I? But not anymore. I have all that I need. Greed is my sustenance, it is all of me and I am all that I dream. I crave what I am. Fuck everyone else. Fuck you."

The tears are now thick, heavy as they hack down through each side of her lovely face. She looks so vulnerable. So confused and wanting. More, but more of what, more love perhaps? Maybe she's never once had it. Not really. Poor thing.

"Fuck you, so funny you should say that. For I have a little tale of my own to tell. Cast your mind back some twenty-two years now. If you would. If you would be so kind. Do you remember a doctor, a scientist named Hing, one Dr Samuel Hing to be most exact? Lovely man, brilliant man. Recently deceased man."

"No, I'm quite sure that I do not."

"Oh, come on, he would have been so unhappy to hear that. Try harder, lean into it. Give your past a little nudge, you can do it."

"Did I fuck him, is that what this is all about? You think you are mine and so lay claim to all that I've got?"

"No, no, Jesus no, but you gave him your eggs and a tasty wee slice of your genes. Those pretty little twisting ladders of yours. You seriously don't remember him, do you? Simply tossed him aside, added him to the heap when he lied and said that his little experiment on your behalf had failed. He wasn't, but I called him Daddy. A very good man sadly missed."

"No way."

"Oh, but hells-the-yes way, and what was the last thing he said to you? Do you remember now, is it all flooding back, as he stood like the whimpering fool in the rain at your door? Like a wet dog, he begged and pleaded with you to love him, did he not? What a fucking loser, right? A good man, but a fucking loser no less."

And I can see in her eyes as she reforms the echo of his words and I am sure she, again, hears the crackle in them as they broke and fell to the floor.

"He told me…" she stutters.

"Yes? Go on, you can do it."

"He told me to go fuck myself."

"He did now, didn't he just? That is exactly what he said. And it's taken a good few years but here we are, clone sweet clone. Such a funny and twisted old world, don't you think?"

What You Wanted

by David Green

Luxar held no regret. Why should he? A vampire desires blood.

He stood before the twelve members of the High Council and bared his fangs when any locked eyes with him. *Pathetic,* he thought with a sneer, *ancient and decrepit. They haven't swum with the thrill of bloodlust in their veins for centuries.*

"Luxar," Nicolu began. The Vampire Elder stood tall above all else. Luxor's defiance lost some of its edge when that black stare fell on him. "You stand accused of the wanton massacre of thirty-seven humans in one night, breaking several of our laws. How do you plead?"

Luxar spread his hands.

"Not guilty, Elder."

The Ancient One's lips curved as he glanced at the council members.

"Explain," he commanded, as his pointed fangs glinted in the candlelight of the massive, underground chamber.

Luxar shrugged and flicked a strand of his white hair

out of his face.

"Humans are cattle. I hungered, so I fed. Each taste of their blood drove me to spill more. My lust urged me until I could drink no more, though if one more human crossed my path that night, I'd have found space for a little extra."

"You admit the crime but plead not guilty?"

"We are better!" Luxar cried, the words bouncing off the walls. "How dare any of you tell me how much I can hunt? You sat in your protected palace, brought blood on platters you haven't spilled yourselves. If any are guilty here, it isn't me."

Luxar panted, his anger getting the better of him. He turned to leave, the desire to hunt strong.

"I did not dismiss you," the Elder Vampire uttered, holding up a hand. Luxar stood rooted to the spot, invisible restraints holding him in place. "Do you regret your greed?"

"No," Luxar snarled as he strained against the unseen barrier. "I take what I want. It's our way."

The Elder Vampire studied him for a second, before turning to each of the High Council. The vampires nodded as Nicolu swept his gaze across them.

"Very well," he spoke. "If blood is what you desire, you'll receive your fill."

Two vampires appeared at Luxar's side, wrenched his jaw open, and jammed a stone funnel between his teeth.

"No," Luxar tried to scream, his eyes wide with panic. He'd seen this punishment before.

The Elder Vampire leaped from the dais and landed in front of Luxar with a grace beyond his years.

"Young vampires never learn," he said, a sly grin on his face. "There is an order to the world. There is no place for greed."

He clapped his hands. An attendant strode towards them, carrying an enormous stone jug. The smell of the liquid inside filled Luxar's nostrils—vampire blood. Drinking but a drop caused illness, a mouthful, an agonising death. The jar contained enough to kill an entire warren of Luxar's kind.

"Luxar," the Elder Vampire announced, placing the jug against the funnel. "I find you guilty and sentence you to your fill of blood. It's what you wanted."

Luxar gagged as the first droplets hit the back of his throat, followed by a continuous rush of liquid cascading into his gullet. He felt it burn as it tore the lining of his stomach, as it mixed with his own bloodstream and made it boil.

Luxar tried to scream as the vampire blood cooked

him from the inside out, but the stream of blood rushing down his throat wouldn't let him. He wanted to fall to the floor, to wail in agony as his organs boiled, but the invisible restraints wouldn't allow it—and still more vampire blood filled his throat.

Luxar stared into the Elder Vampire's cruel, smiling face until his eyeballs exploded from his body's heat. When the stench of his own sizzling skin entered his nose, he knew he'd soon be ash, and he'd want for blood no longer.

No Transplant for Dexter

by Stephen Herczeg

Marlon Schutter stood and stared at the frail form lying on the hospital bed before him. Tubes ran in and out of the grey-haired old man, connecting him to the life-saving machinery that surrounded the bed. Beeps, whirrs, and pings echoed around the room. A thin green line crossed the screen of the electrocardiogram, jumping every second in comforting regularity. Marlon shook his head in sorrow.

You bloody idiot.

The potential corpse was Dexter Ridley, owner of DexCom, the fastest growing corporation in the country. A simple business germinated in a small country town but driven purely by the inner need of its owner, a desire to consume other businesses and bring their assets and wealth into its own. All consuming, all powerful. Dexter's secret had always been diversity. Diversity of thought. Diversity of products. Diversity of customer.

Over the years, Dexter had implemented a plan to

grow faster through increased acquisitions. Any business that came into his sights was quickly and efficiently absorbed. Sometimes through simple, patient ways, sometimes through other means less palatable to right thinking minds.

Marlon had assisted Dexter for over ten years. He'd clawed his way up through the company ranks and spent his working life dedicated to one organisation, something rare in the modern era, but part of his plan. Marlon was committed to Dexter and DexCom itself, though he hid his true desires from view. Externally he was a patient man, willing to dedicate himself to his boss in every way possible. Internally, he waited for the opportunity he hoped would finally be his to take.

Recently, his plans began to reach fruition.

Dexter's work allowed no time or space for marriage or the siring of children. He had often voiced his regret to Marlon but admitted that family would only be an annoyance and distraction from his life's purpose—that of growing his business and making it the largest entity on Earth.

A month previously, Dexter had called Marlon into his office and told him to sit. A rare event in their relationship. Marlon's mind raced with worry. Thoughts ran of some slight or wrong decision he'd made. Sensing his distress, Dexter calmed him down before pushing a sheaf of legal papers towards him.

"Sign these," Dexter said. "I want you to become my power of attorney, in case anything happens to me. You'll have authority to make decisions for me, in the event I become incapacitated. You will also have control over any medical judgements that need to be made on my behalf."

Marlon played it cool, appearing to read the text carefully, while internally squealing and picturing himself jumping for joy on Dexter's grave. Finally, after the requisite few minutes, he signed the documents and passed them back.

"I'll never need this though, will I?" he asked, innocently.

"I hope not," Dexter replied. "But, I'm getting old and this body is wearing out."

Just as Marlon reached the exit, his brain exploding at his sudden turn of fortune, Dexter finished with a thought that crushed Marlon's exhilaration. "Of course, if I die, then it all means nothing anyway," he said.

Marlon stared at the hypnotic green line as it traced its path across the black, circular screen. He almost found himself willing it to continue, forever. As long as Dexter lay in his current state, Marlon was in command. If the line flattened, he had nothing.

A white-gown-wearing doctor entered the room. After a cursory check of the chart and machines, he turned to Marlon and shrugged. "It was a full coronary attack. The heart suffered extreme trauma. The only thing keeping Mr Ridley alive is the machines."

Marlon's face dropped. "Transplant?"

The doctor shook his head. "I'm sorry. He's too old. His health has been too poor for too long to be even considered for a replacement. You need to decide when to turn off the switch."

Marlon's memory stepped back several hours as he pictured the final moments before Dexter succumbed.

It was another business deal. A large company. The company sold nothing out of the ordinary but had become the focus of Dexter's desire for months, and what Dexter wanted, Dexter always managed to get.

The telephone conversation with the company's owner had become heated. Dexter raged and swore into the phone. Marlon watched as the vein on Dexter's forehead throbbed and pulsed as his face grew red. With one last outburst, Dexter's voice froze, his hand grabbed at his chest, his eyes bulged. The phone dropped to the desk, followed by Dexter.

Marlon sighed. All his plans had come to naught.

Dexter would be dead within days and he could only prolong it for so long. All the power thrown his way with a simple signature would evaporate when the green line straightened.

A jiggle in his pocket snapped his attention back to reality. He snatched out his phone and answered without taking note of the number.

"Yes?"

"Mr Schutter?"

"Yes, who is this? What do you want?"

"Mr Schutter, I represent Clorax Industries, one of DexCom's subsidiary companies. One of DexCom's *health industry* related companies."

"So?"

"We understand that Mr Ridley has suffered a coronary arrest, and he has been denied a transplant."

"Bad news travels fast."

A slight chuckle at the other end of the phone was followed by "Yes. Yes, it does. But it doesn't all have to end badly."

Intrigued, Marlon continued, "Okay, now you've got my attention, be quick."

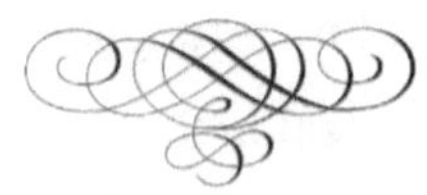

Marlon opened the door to Dexter's office and

entered quietly. He crept softly across the tiles and stood within metres of the large oak desk.

Dexter paced before the large window that afforded him a wondrous view of the city stretching out before him. The city in which he personally held the lives of hundreds of thousands of residents in his hands. Dexter's voice was highly animated, more amusing and joyous than Marlon had known for years. He finished the call with a happy agreement between himself and the caller. Another deal done. Another company purchased. Another notch on his belt.

As Dexter turned to face him, Marlon felt uneasy, an emotional state becoming more familiar since the operation. His boss had recovered beyond even Marlon's expectations and certainly beyond his desire. Instead of a vegetable that would lay in a coma for years to come, Dexter had almost bounced off the operating table when the mechanical heart was first activated. Since then, he had stripped off the weight and was virtually a new man, with an even greater vitality to inject into his ambitions.

Marlon, himself, was a wreck. Dexter's newfound energy drained him. He simply couldn't keep up with the tasks Dexter threw at him throughout the day and night.

"Marlon," Dexter said, "I have a new plan." A wide smile spread across his face, filling Marlon with dread.

"And you are going to help me achieve it."

"Yes, sir?" Marlon's thin voice was almost lost in the large office.

"I want to live forever. No"—Dexter thumped the desk—"I must live forever." Dexter's grin became a malevolent sneer. "Because how else will I grow my empire to embrace the whole world?"

Doctor Barton McFinch looked at Marlon Schutter's exasperated face. "Mr Schutter, relax, I assure you Mr Ridley is in the best of health for someone his age," he said.

"What the hell did you people do to him on that operating table? He's gone insane." Marlon pushed the piece of paper before him across the desk. "This is his list of demands. He wants to replace every organ, bone, and muscle in his body with mechanical parts."

Barton picked up the page and scanned it. "Interesting." The smile remained, as he ticked off the items that could be achieved in his head and added the costs of research and development required to invent the others. Clorax was one of the most advanced companies in the medical industry, but even they were years away from developing the sort of technology that Dexter Ridley was after.

Finally, Barton looked up from the list. "Most of this is purely fantasy at this stage…" Marlon tried to interrupt, but Barton spoke over him, "But, if Mr Ridley is willing to support our research and development efforts, then within decades, perhaps even years, we could be in a situation where most of these requests are actually possible."

"How much money?"

Barton nonchalantly ran his eyes over the list again, biding his time before answering. He peered back at Marlon, his smile slightly wider. "I certainly couldn't put a hard figure on it, but we are talking billions."

Marlon's mouth dropped open.

"Just to start with," Barton continued. "Of course, it depends on Mr Ridley's intentions." Barton leaned forward, held out a hand, and slowly closed it into a fist. His grin turned into a sneer as he spoke. "How many more years he wants to wrench from his body or how many more companies he wants to hold in his hands? It's all up to him."

"Look, it's simple. I want your company. You undertake medical research that will complement my own company's research. You also have products that I want to use." Marlon stood patiently in his regular spot and watched Dexter converse with the air. Dexter's implanted communications device negating the need for a handset. "My offer stands. Have a think about it. I already have the majority of your shareholders on board, but I'm trying to be a nice guy here. Okay? I'll call you in the morning." Dexter placed a robotic finger to his temple to disengage the call.

Marlon was surprised when Dexter finally noticed him. The blank mask of his plastic face hid any emotion. "Marlon?" he said, his eyeballs whirring as they changed focus. "You're looking old."

Marlon peered down at his hands: the wrinkled skin announced his age to the world. He flexed his hand into a fist. The pain in his arthritic joints confirming how old he had become. Finally, he replied, "I am old. It's been twenty years since you started this replacement campaign. You get younger with each operation, while mere mortals like me continue the slow decline."

A strange clucking noise emanated from the speaker array that now served as Dexter's voice box. They still hadn't successfully emulated laughter.

"Chin up, my friend, once I'm complete, we might be able to start work on you," Dexter said.

The thought of turning into a bastardised human mechanoid hybrid, like the one standing before him, filled Marlon with dread. His optimism of outliving this man was fading by the day, but he still hoped he could see him fall and take over the reins of the company.

"What was your call about?" he asked to change the subject.

"That idiot Xu Lin from Wuhan Enterprises. He won't sell. They've developed a new biofuel filtration system which Clorax could use to replace my digestive tract." His hand grasped at his midriff. Marlon knew Dexter's stomach was riddled with ulcers from his high-stress life and was close to failing. Dexter recovered and placed a metallic hand to his plastic face. "And they've developed a facial replacement system that has defined musculature. I want that system. I want to show emotion again. It's too hard to get my point across to the idiots I have to deal with if they can't see it in my eyes."

He strode around the desk towards Marlon. His heavy footsteps clacking on the tiled floor. That emotionless plastic face moved in close to Marlon's. Internally, he was repelled, but he held firm.

"I need you to organise *the boys* to pay a visit. Softly at first. If he still won't sell, then they can take it up a notch."

The boys were Dexter's goon squad, used to ensure that business deals went smoothly, mostly through aggravated violence against family members. Xu Lin was in for a heap of trouble.

"Marlon," the disembodied voice floated out of the throat speaker, "I want this. I want that company; I want that technology, and nothing will stop me getting it."

Marlon stared into the emotionless plastic face. He knew his place and nodded silently. "I'll report back when it's done." He turned and left, cursing inside but reminding himself to hold firm.

One day it will pay off.

Marlon waved his hand at the viewing area above his desk. Several reports materialised and floated side by side. Each detailed the latest company acquisitions. DexCom was finally the largest of its kind in the world. Dexter had achieved his dream, in more ways than one.

One final report floated into view. It was from Clorax Industries. McFinch had delivered the final product in a long history of initiatives begun by Dexter more than four decades before. Marlon read the report and chuckled. Clorax had managed to replicate the human brain in synthetic form. The unit could download the thoughts, memories, even dreams of the host and could be linked in with all the mechanical systems developed for Dexter so far.

The last piece of the puzzle.

The report stated that the operation was a total success. Dexter had entered the hospital the previous day, undergone the surgical replacement, and left before nightfall. A new man. A new creation. A new species. Totally synthetic.

Marlon smiled to himself.

His office door opened, and a small rat-like man entered.

"Cyrum? What can I do for you?"

Cyrum Fernley, the company's lawyer, stood at the threshold holding an ancient paper folder in his hand. "Um, I'm sorry to disturb you, Mr Schutter, but Mr Ridley asked me to see you."

"About?"

Cyrum approached the desk, lay the folder down, and opened it. Marlon saw the top sheet of paper it contained and chuckled inside. It was the power of attorney document that he had signed forty years previously.

"My Lord, I thought that this had been lost years ago." He looked into the lawyer's eyes. "What is this about then?"

"Mr Ridley needs you to sign it back to him. He said he doesn't need it anymore. Something about finally being immortal."

Marlon smiled; he had expected this day to come. As soon as he was able, Dexter would rip back any power that he had given out. This document was the key to all that. Marlon played along and fished out an old-fashion pen from his desk drawer. He'd kept it specifically for this moment and hoped it still worked. Hiding his intent, he drew circles on the folder itself to get the ink running again. As he hovered over the release signature block, he peered up at Cyrum. "What do you know about Mr Ridley's last will and testament?"

Cyrum brightened. "Oh, quite a lot actually. I read it again only two days ago, just before his operation. Um, just in case."

Marlon smiled. "What does it say about suicide?"

Cyrum was taken aback. He thought for a moment before answering. "Um, it states that in the event of suicide, the will is null and void, and all responsibilities revert back to the Power of Attorney." The little man's face showed confusion. "Why?"

"What is suicide? From the legal perspective?"

"Um, the deliberate forfeiture of one's life by one's own hand."

"And what is the legal definition of life?"

The little man's face scrunched up in thought. "Um, the aggregate of all *animal* functions which resist death."

"So, if a person willingly removes all *animal* functions from themselves, what would that be?"

Cyrum's eyes grew wider, his mouth dropped open, "Oh, my Lord."

Marlon smiled widely. "Precisely."

"Marlon?" Dexter turned at the sound of the door. Marlon noticed Dexter stood in his familiar position watching the rain sprinkle down on his empire beyond the large view windows, as if he were a king and all around were merely peasants ready to command at will.

I wonder if he wants to control the weather next.

Marlon shuffled over, leaning heavily on his cane, his arthritic hips on fire as the damp weather had rolled in. He placed the manilla folder on his boss' desk. "Cyrum visited me this morning with this."

Dexter peered at the folder. His newly installed facial mechanics giving him the haunting look of his younger self staring out from a mechanoid body, enhanced with the ability to express emotions. His face split into a smile. "You've signed it then?"

"No. I will. I just have some questions first."

Dexter padded around the desk, a recent upgrade to his leg suspension dulling his footsteps. "Yes?"

"I've been a willing assistant for over forty years. Witnessed many *things*. I'd like to retire in comfort, but…" He let the words hang for effect.

Dexter's synthetic face worked overtime as the rage flowed through. "What? After all this time you're asking for more money?" Dexter stalked around the room, the sound of metal thumping into plastic split the silence as he slapped a hand against his chest. "I built this empire. Me. It's all mine. I will not let any of it slip away. Sign and leave while you still can. Or…" He stepped up and poked Marlon in the chest. "*The boys* might pay *you* a visit."

Marlon simply smiled. "I thought you'd see it that way." He drew his hand out of his pocket, aimed, and pulled the trigger of the taser he held.

Thousands of volts flew into his robotic boss. Dexter jumped and danced across the floor, before collapsing in a smoking heap. His eyes managed to turned towards Marlon, grinding as they focused on him.

"You've killed me," a dry, rattling voice emanated from the throat speaker before all went dead.

"That's the beauty of it all, I didn't need to, you

already killed yourself."

He pressed a finger to his temple.

"Maintenance, this is Mr Schutter, I have a broken machine that needs removing from Mr Ridley's office."

Fated Riches

by J.W. Garrett

The flutter of something brushed her cheek, whisper soft but there. She jolted at the movement, her face now blazing from the touch. Camille's eyes blinked opened. Ahead, a line formed into the horizon and beyond. From her spot at the end, nothing was visible. She tapped the person ahead of her. "Sorry, but what—"

Camille's mouth fell open. One of the woman's eyes had been gouged out, and an angry wound oozed from her stomach. "I…I…" Dread snaked a path through Camille, as she held her breath and let her gaze drift slowly over her own body. Her hand slid down her neck, coming back wet, drenched in blood. "What happened to me?" she murmured. "Am I dead?"

"Looks that way to me," the one-eyed lady answered, "but I'm waiting to find out why I'm here, same as you."

Standing on tiptoe, Camille arched her neck for a better view. "That's pointless. You'll just have to hang out, like the rest of us."

Even though Camille's wounds weren't painful, the fear in her middle grew. The last she could remember, she and her husband had returned from a late dinner and were retiring for the night. Besides that, nothing was clear—her head a hazy mess of fragmented thoughts.

How? When? Those questions needed answers, but time seemed to have no meaning here—wherever *here* was. A minute or an hour later—anyone's guess—when the crowd dissipated, Camille lifted her head to a beautiful winged creature. So close, she could seemingly reach out and touch one of the fluffy feathers adorning the angel. But, as before, the distance was distorted. He was hopelessly beyond her grasp, and only he and Camille were here now.

She didn't speak, her eyes averted, waiting for him to instead. The ridged lines of his jaw and his lips set in a thin line didn't foreshadow good news, as the man perused a digital readout.

"Seems to be a small problem. Your net data tally is inconclusive." The being cocked his head. "Not enough definitive information to support a decision either way. Unusual, but not unheard of."

Camille met his stormy gaze. "So, I am dead?"

"Not in the truest sense of how you mean the word. You're in a purgatory of sorts. That's the easiest way for you to grasp your current state. One from which you can still return to the world of the living for a time. Remember this?" he asked, pulling a necklace out of thin air.

Camille swallowed hard, reaching for her prized possession. But like everything else here, she couldn't quite get to it. The beautiful black diamond jewels swayed in and out of her vision, teasing her—the motion mesmerising.

In his alternate hand, he clutched other pieces of jewellery…all hers.

"Give them to me. Please," she begged. "They're mine. I need them."

"Not letting this go"—the angel let the shimmering stones slide from his fingers into nothingness—"is how you got that death wound on your neck. But you lost something much more precious in that encounter also."

"I remember now," she answered, her eyes still searching where her jewels had been. "My husband died."

The angel nodded. "Yes. Trying to protect you. So you'll have one final test, another opportunity, before a decision is rendered. And you'll remember none of what has just transpired between us. Your actions will determine placement. Choose wisely."

His hand sliced the air, and she stumbled, falling, spinning out of control, careening through an endless sea of darkness.

Camille stared at her necklace in the mirror, admiring the sparkle as she moved, the black diamonds stealing the light. A shudder rippled through her, and she staggered, reaching for the dresser to keep from falling.

"Are you all right?" Dustin moved to her side, offering a steadying hand.

"Yes. I adore my beautiful necklace. I can't take my eyes off it."

"*Mmm*. There are better visions to appreciate in the room… Take it off and come to bed," he said, tugging her with him.

"No…I think I'll leave it on. I just can't bear to part with it for the night." She lingered, watching the reflection play with the light. "Matching earrings would be just the thing. Don't you think so?"

"You have plenty of earrings in your drawers full of priceless treasures. Pick something out. Later."

"But I really *need* the ones that go with this," she whined.

"We'll see." He chuckled. "Soon my clothes will have no room in the closet. Your jewellery boxes will take up that space."

"Now—"

Glass shattered into their bedroom.

"Hurry, Camille, into the panic room!" Dustin tossed

her behind him, as he confronted a masked intruder. Camille took a hurried step towards her shelter, glanced backward at the mounds of defenceless jewels on her dresser, and dashed into the room again.

A man held her husband, a knife pressed against his neck.

"Dustin!"

"Camille…Go…" he pleaded.

Camille eyed her goal, darted to her gems, and grabbed two handfuls. Taking a slow step backwards, she held the stranger's gaze.

The man loosed a maniacal laugh. "Nah…No, you don't." He waved her forward. "Hand over that necklace you're wearing. Now!"

Camille inched another step backward, shaking her head.

"If I have to come get it, he dies. Then you." With a quick twist, the robber dug the knifepoint into Dustin's neck.

In a sudden burst of energy, Dustin freed an elbow and slammed it into the man's face.

Frozen in place, Camille clutched her necklace. "No, you can't have it. You can't," she whispered.

A wicked smile crossed the man's lips as he regained control, opened Dustin's throat, and dropped the body.

The intruder closed the distance to Camille in three short steps. "This is your doing. *You* had a choice here."

Camille's gaze homed in on the grisly scene, as her husband fought for his last breath.

"I always keep my promises." The intruder yanked the necklace free and carved a red smile across Camille's throat, to match her husband's.

"Your desire for pieces of jewellery, which you've set above all else, is clear. You shall have them be your eternal company."

Camille lifted her gaze to the beautiful, winged creature, his face lined in sadness. "I remember. I've been here before, in a long line."

"Yes." He nodded slowly. "No waiting this time around."

"My husband…where is he?"

"Up ahead." The angel gestured to a cobblestone path, leading to a massive door.

"Let me see him."

The being shook his head. "I'm afraid not. A decision has been rendered. Follow me."

Camille trailed him on a broken path, covered with thorns and rocks. "Here."

A door whooshed open, revealing a twisting set of stairs spiralling below to an end she couldn't see. "Wait. There must be another way."

"No. This is the only way for you and your jewellery to spend eternity together." The angel walked away, shedding a feather. Transfixed, Camille snatched it from its lazy descent through the air.

"But…" Stuck in place, her feet sank deeper into the path, as she strained to follow the disappearing set of wings. Spinning to face her fate, Camille plunged forward, her legs like anchors, plodding down the only path available to her. Finally, her feet perched on the first step, she gasped for breath, still clinging to the feather. Holding the white plume in front of her like a beacon, Camille took a slow, shaky step.

As she inched forward again, it fell from her hand in a burst of flames.

Fortune

by Jodi Jensen

"What does your fortune say?"

In keeping with the Friday night ritual, Jade broke open her cookie. She paused with bated breath as she looked around the table, waiting until she had the full attention of her friends. "A very attractive person has a message for you."

"Oooooh, girl, look at you!" Her best friend, Nola, slapped the tabletop and joined in with the whistles and catcalls from the rest of the group.

Snickering, Jade tucked the slip of paper in her pocket. "Okay, all right, settle down now. Who's next?"

"Wait, wait—" Nola gasped, choking back her laughter. "Don't you want your message? I've got it right here." She held up both middle fingers, then collapsed against her chair in peals of giggles.

The other girls around the table erupted in hilarity.

"She *is* pretty damn fine—"

"Very fine—"

"—you like *that* message?"

"Oh, fuck off, all of you, that hurts." Despite her best

effort to feign offence, Jade burst out laughing.

The five of them had known each other since high school, and between them, they conquered college, more hook-ups and breakups than she could count, and all shared the same raunchy sense of humour.

After they'd gone around the table, everyone sharing their fortunes in a similar fashion, they split the bill and called it a night.

Everyone except Jade. Before heading home, she had a stop to make first.

As was her own personal custom, she always bought a lottery ticket with the numbers off her fortune cookie. She'd won a few bucks here and there, but nothing to get excited about. Not yet, anyway.

Deciding to try a whole new place, she stopped at a round-the-clock gas station for tonight's ticket. When she walked in, her gaze collided with a tall, raven-haired, sexy-as-fuck cashier with bedroom eyes, and her fortune came to mind. This guy certainly fit the bill of a *very attractive person*, so flashing him her best flirty grin, she picked up a lottery sheet, filled it out, and got in his line.

"What can I do for you?" he asked.

She nearly swooned at the rich timbre of his voice. "Just the lottery ticket"—she peeked at his nametag— "Mason, and I picked my own numbers."

He grinned and a dimple flashed in his right cheek. "Yes, ma'am."

"Name's Jade." She giggled. "Not ma'am."

"I like that." Lips still turned up in a smile, he took the play sheet. "Three dollars, Jade." He took her money and turned, scanning her ticket. Before giving her back her play sheet, he scribbled something on a yellow sticky note, then handed them both over with a wink. "Good luck."

Once outside, she looked at what he'd written. *Score!* She climbed into her car, tapped out a text to Mason, then cranked the music as she pulled away.

It was going to be a great night.

The next evening, Jade tuned in to see if she'd had any luck with her lottery ticket. While she waited, she texted Mason to see what he was up to.

"Ah, here we go," she muttered, glancing at the television as the weekly lottery drawing began. She popped the top off a beer as the host called out the number twenty-five.

Got one! She hit send on the text to Mason, then took a swig of her drink.

Woooo! came the swift reply.

She giggled as her thumbs flew over her screen. *Don't get too excited, didn't win anything yet.*

When the host called out the number forty-five next, her heart sped up a fraction.

Got another one!

Now we're talking! The thumbs-up emoji that followed his message made her roll her eyes.

Scooting to the edge of the couch, she kept her gaze glued to the TV as another ball was drawn. Thirty-two, not one of her numbers.

Damn, streak is over.

Least you won something, I never do.

"Not even ten bucks," she mumbled. But then the number twelve was called, and she grinned as she glanced at her ticket.

Ooooooh, three out of four!

How much is that?

Don't know yet.

The last one drawn was a bust, but then the host called the bonus number, eighteen, and she realised she'd won a hundred dollars. She couldn't help but think how lucky her last fortune cookie had been as she shot another text off to Mason.

Enough to buy dinner tomorrow, you in?

Where?

This rockin' little Chinese place I know.

Eh, Idk, not really my thing.

She frowned at her phone. Maybe he wasn't as interested as she'd thought? *It's where I get my lottery numbers.*

Oooo count me in.

"Yeah, that's what I thought," she mumbled, setting her phone aside. In the past, her fortunes had been good to her, giving her on-point guidance in life, though she'd never won anything with the lotto. She just needed to keep the faith, she decided, as she glanced at the clock.

Shit! Jumping up, she made a dash for the bathroom. She had just enough time for a shower before her night shift at the club.

Dinner the next day went well, and though Mason didn't eat much, his interest in her seemed to have gone up a few notches. So, why was she so nervous?

"You first." She batted her eyes at him.

"Nah, ladies first," he insisted with a nod at the fortune cookie in her hand.

She hesitated, took a deep breath, then broke the cookie open. Keeping her gaze on him, she fingered the tiny slip of paper.

"Well? What's it say?"

Suddenly, she didn't want to know, but as she stared into the depths of his warm brown eyes, she found she couldn't deny him. She cleared her throat and glanced down. "The greatest risk is not taking one."

His face split into a wide grin. "I don't usually buy into stuff like this, but I've got an idea." Shoving his own cookie aside, untouched, he slid out of the booth and held his hand out. "C'mon. Let's go take a risk."

A surge of excitement pulsed through her. This was the kind of guy she liked: spur-of-the-moment, unpredictable, and fun. He even surprised her by paying the bill.

Outside, they got into his beater of a car, and he drove to the nearest gas station.

"Go grab some scratch tickets." He held up a fifty-dollar bill, but when she went to grab it, he pulled his arm back. "Halves on whatever we win, deal?"

"Deal." She grinned as she snatched the bill from him and hopped out of the car. A moment later, she was back with a handful of tickets, and they took turns scratching them off. When they were finished, she took them back inside to be scanned.

As the cashier tallied their winnings, Jade kept her gaze glued to the running total. Unable to contain herself, she giggled and bounced on her tiptoes when the final number showed over five hundred dollars in winnings.

Once she'd collected the money, she half-ran, half-skipped to the car, waving the bills at Mason. "Can you believe this?"

"How much?" His face lit up, and he leaned over the gear shifter and reached for the cash.

This time, she was the one to pull her arm back. "Geez greedy, hang on a sec." Sliding in the passenger side, she slammed the door shut, then spread the pile of twenties out on her lap. "Five hundred and twelve dollars." She flashed him a grin and divided the money.

"What ya going to do with your half?" he asked, stuffing his bills into his pocket.

She rolled her eyes at him. "Buy more tickets, of course. You?"

"Same," he chuckled and shook his head, "but later. I gotta get my ass to work now."

Too busy dreaming of winning more cash, she didn't notice or think to care that he never even kissed her goodbye when he dropped her off in front of her building.

The next afternoon, Jade called the Chinese restaurant for an order of take-out. She thought about texting Mason to see if he wanted some, but decided against it. He hadn't seemed to care much for the food, or her company, if she was being honest. It was her luck he wanted in on.

"Don't forget my fortune cookie," she said, after placing her order.

"Would you like a few extra?"

She considered briefly, but realised a single cookie hadn't steered her wrong yet, so she'd better stick with what was working. "Nah, just the one, and I'll pay when it's delivered."

After verifying her address, she hurried to get cleaned up. She had just enough time to shower and twist her damp hair into a hasty braid, when there was a knock at her door.

"Damn, that was fast." She opened the door and her jaw dropped.

"You think you're doing this without me?" Mason stood in the hall, holding her takeout bag.

"What the hell, dude?" She stepped forward and reached for her food. "That's mine."

He jerked his arm back, holding the white paper sack out of her reach. "I paid for it, you gonna let me in or what?"

"Wha... How..."

"How'd I know?" His lips twisted in a sneer. "Did you forget you told me this is how you get your lottery numbers?"

She sighed and, against her better judgement, let him in. "I'm only doing this because I want my cookie."

"Oh, I know that." He shrugged as he stepped over the threshold. "You're as greedy as I am, greedier probably, seeing as how you didn't even invite me after last night's winnings." Holding the bag just out of her reach, he added, "Partners, right? From here on out."

She scowled and gave him a sharp nod.

"Say it," he demanded. "Partners."

"Partners," she hissed between gritted teeth. "Now, give it here."

He finally handed the bag over and plopped himself on a barstool in her tiny one-room apartment. "Let's get to it."

Fucking jerk! She gave him what she hoped was a dirty look. "There's a routine to this, you know. Eat first, then the cookie."

"Don't let me stop you, then." He folded his arms across his chest and shot a pointed glance at the bag. "Eat up."

Refusing to sit near him, she went to the couch and spread her food on the coffee table. She deliberately ate slow, partly because he was glowering the entire time and she enjoyed prodding him, and partly because he made her more nervous than she was comfortable with.

When she finally finished, she picked up the cookie and broke it open. She closed her eyes for a few seconds, then peered at the slip of paper.

Her heart skipped a beat and she smiled.

You already know the answer to the questions lingering inside your head.

"Well?"

"Huh?" She jumped at the sharply spoken word. "Oh, this one's not so helpful."

"Let me see."

Without turning to look at him, she held the paper over her shoulder.

"The fuck does that mean?" he demanded a few seconds later.

"Told you." She shrugged and got up, stuffing the remnants of her food back into the sack. "Guess we're skipping this one."

"No."

She turned to see him studying her with a frown.

"It means you're picking the place to buy the tickets this time. And you can pay, too."

"Is that so?" She planted her feet apart and glared at

him.

"Says right there, you already know the answer, so yeah, that's how it's gonna be."

She looked away and headed to the trashcan with her garbage. Let him think what he wanted; he didn't need to know what the message meant to *her*. "Whatever."

"Whatever my ass. Grab your crap and let's go."

"What? Right now? I'm not ready to go anywhere, I look like shit."

"No one cares." He waved a hand at the door. "I don't have all damn day."

"Jackass," she muttered under her breath.

"What'd you say?"

"Nothing." She snatched her purse from the counter and stalked to the door.

"That's what I thought."

Wishing she could wipe the smug look from his stupid face, she locked up and followed him to his car.

"Wanna tell me what we're doing here?" Mason had pulled into the parking lot at her direction and glanced at the building. "They sell scratch tickets?"

Jade stifled a giggle. "Everywhere sells scratch tickets." She reached for the door handle. "I'll be right back."

He grabbed her arm. "No monkey business."

Jerking away, she got out, slammed the door, and headed inside the *Carnival Emporium*. Half-museum, half-tourist shop, it did indeed offer scratch tickets for sale, but she had a quick stop to make first.

She headed to the back of the shop, and sure enough, just as her friend Nola had mentioned once, right across from the bathrooms was a small room with strings of beads hanging in the doorway. Ducking inside, Jade pulled her wallet out and slapped a twenty down on the table, where a dark-haired woman sat in an over-the-top clichéd fortune teller costume. "I'd like my fortune, please."

The woman raised an eyebrow. "Palm reading, tarot, or crystal ball?"

"Crystal ball"—Jade glanced over her shoulder, then back at the woman—"and make it quick."

Nodding, the woman waved her hands over the ball in the centre of the table. After a brief moment, she looked at Jade, a slow smile spreading across her thin lips. "You learn from your mistakes… You will learn a lot over the next few days."

Another affirmation I've got to do something about Mason, as if I needed one.

"Thank you." She smiled warmly at the woman. "That's more helpful than you know."

The woman reached under the table and came out with a small vial. "If you want helpful, take this." She shook the vial, rattling the contents. "Ground castor bean seeds. Don't *you* eat them."

Accepting the gift with a nod, Jade left the room and hurried up front to buy the scratch tickets.

As before, she and Mason sat in the car and scratched all the tickets—this time a hundred dollars' worth, then she took them back inside to be scanned. She wasn't even surprised when the winnings totalled nearly eight hundred today.

Rather than dividing the money evenly, Mason decided he'd take more since he paid for her food. Once he'd subtracted the cost of the tickets, she got a measly two-fifty, which was slightly less than last night's haul.

Anger burned in her gut when he dropped her off in front of her building.

"No funny stuff," he ordered, giving her a hard look. "I'll be back tomorrow and we'll do the same."

"Yessir." She mock-saluted him, then turned, and marched away, fuming.

Later that night, she ordered take-out again. Not for the lottery numbers or scratch ticket luck, but for some personal insight. When the delivery came, she brushed aside the food and went straight for the cookie.

Fortune favours the brave.

She paced her tiny apartment, thinking. *I already have the answer to my question, I'm going to learn a lot, and I need to be brave.* Ideas swirled in her mind, mixing with the three fortunes.

Wait…

In order to learn a lot, I have to be brave. And I've got my answer already.

She grinned as a plan hatched.

The next day, Mason showed up at noon sharp, and Jade was ready.

"Let's both order today," she said as she let him in.

"I don't want anything. Besides, all we really need is your cookie."

"We never even looked at yours that time in the restaurant, maybe it'll double our luck." She glanced at him, trying to gage his reaction and decided he didn't look convinced. "Just get some soup, you don't have to eat it. I love it. I'll stick it in the fridge and save it for later."

"Whatever." He shrugged as he made himself comfortable on her couch.

After placing the order, she got out a beer and handed it to him.

He looked surprised, but accepted and chugged it.

Smiling, she got him another one.

By the time the food arrived, he'd downed three beers and excused himself to use the bathroom.

Perfect!

Knowing she only had a moment, she retrieved the vial she'd been given yesterday and dumped it in the soup.

"What's that?"

She startled and her heart about jumped out of her chest. "Nothing—seasoning, that's all."

Mason stared at her for a second, then erupted from where he stood, crossing the room in two steps. He grabbed her by the hair and yanked her head back. "Then you drink it," he roared, dumping the soup down her throat.

Struggling, she coughed and sputtered, but swallowed a good portion. He released her with a jerk, and she fell to the floor, snot and tears running down her face.

He picked up both cookies and threw them at her. "Read them," he ordered.

Hand shaking, she broke open the first one.

Our deeds determine us as much as we determine our deeds.

She choked on a sob and picked up the other cookie.

Greed doesn't open doors, it closes them.

"Serves you right, you greedy little bitch." He picked up the other bowl of soup and drank it down, then wiped a hand across his mouth. "Not bad at all."

"No, it serves *you* right," she cackled. "Both bowls were poisoned. I knew if I told you how much I liked the soup, you'd want it all for yourself."

The blood drained from his face as he fell to his knees.

She curled into a ball, her back to him, and smiled in spite of the pain. The fortune cookies never let her down.

Azaroth

by G. Allen Wilbanks

Azaroth strolled casually through the diner, hands in his pockets, eyeing the various patrons as they wolfed down their greasy fare or chatted amiably with companions. The business was busy, although not packed. Several empty booths were still available, their tables wiped clean, and new napkins and silverware laid out for the next customers to arrive. Azaroth was not searching for an empty seat, however. He was seeking something, or rather someone, more specific. To his relief, he did not need to search long.

Alone in one of the dining booths slumped a man who had clearly seen more pleasant days. Dejection and defeat were clear in every curved line of his broken posture, as well as in the dull, flat look in his eyes. Though this man was only in his mid-thirties, he looked much older. Time and circumstance had not been kind to him. The man had long, unkempt brown hair, fading to grey, that hung over his pallid features as he stared down at the remains on his plate: a wilted leaf of lettuce, a pickle spear, and a few crumbs of bread that had, five minutes earlier, been a bacon cheeseburger.

Azaroth sat down and slid across the red vinyl bench to centre himself at the lacquered wood table across from his selected target. The man startled and looked up at the new arrival, curiosity and suspicion wrinkling his brow and narrowing his eyes. In return, Azaroth smiled a friendly greeting.

"Hello, Robert. Please do not let me interrupt your meal. Although, it appears you may already be finished eating."

The man Azaroth identified as Robert glowered more deeply. "I don't know you," he said darkly.

"No, of course, you don't. But I know you, Robert. In point of fact, I know you quite well. I know you do not like how people view you as their inferior merely because you make less money than they do. I know you are angry at the women who have treated you like dirt, looking down their noses at you and not giving you so much as a moment of their time because your clothing is old and worn out. I know you wish you could afford to move out of your tiny apartment, the one located at 2452 Guardian Way. Apartment 14B, I believe? And, I also know you despise your landlord, a vicious little man who constantly harasses you to tell you your rent is late, despite the fact he is charging twice what that disgusting rathole is worth."

Robert obviously did not like having a stranger know so much about him, particularly his home address. He stared at Azaroth, his back curved and his shoulders hunched defensively, trying to figure out what this unwelcome newcomer wanted from him.

"I don't know what you think you're doing here, but I suggest you get back up and leave before I decide I should beat your ass into the pavement outside."

Azaroth pressed his lips tightly together and shook his head, disappointed at the blustering response.

"Now, Robert, is that any way to speak to the person who is here to make all your dreams come true?"

"What are you? Some kind of loan shark or something? You gonna loan me some money so I can pay my rent, but then break my legs later when I can't pay you back? No thanks. I have enough problems without adding you to the list."

"I am not here to give you a loan," assured Azaroth. "I am here to offer you a gift. A gift with no expectations of repayment and no strings attached. You may think of me as your own private genie since I am here fully prepared to grant you your fondest wish."

Azaroth smiled broadly at the pronouncement, flashing a mouthful of disturbingly sharp, pointed teeth.

Robert unconsciously leaned back in his seat, putting as much distance between himself and his uninvited guest as possible.

"What the fuck…?" Robert began, but stopped himself when he realised he was shouting. He glanced around, seeing if anyone had noticed his outburst, then lowered his voice once more. "What are you? Are you just some kind of nutjob that gets off on messing with people, or are you honestly claiming you're the Devil?"

"Oh, that is very flattering of you to suggest—but no, there is only one Devil, and I am most assuredly not him. I am just a demon, and quite a minor one at that, although I do have the power to help people if they let me. Like yourself, for instance. I was strolling by, smelled the desperation wafting out of this particular booth, and I decided to sit down and make you a very happy man."

Anger flashed across Robert's face, and for a moment, it appeared as if he might reach across the table and grab Azaroth by his shirt collar. The demon braced himself, but the moment passed. Robert's features relaxed, and he actually began to laugh.

"I think you're crazy. I don't know why you're playing this little game of yours, but I'm not going to play it with you. Even if you were a demon—and I can't believe I'm saying this—but even if you were, there's no way I'm going to sell you my soul for money."

Azaroth and Robert were interrupted by an older woman in a pink dress and white apron stepping up to their table. She waited until they acknowledged her presence, then leaned in apologetically.

"Excuse me, guys, but can I get you anything else?" She had a pleasant voice, with a soft southern US accent. Azaroth guessed she must have grown up somewhere around Mississippi or Alabama. "Would you like to order some dessert this afternoon? We have a really nice homemade peach cobbler."

"No," Robert told her. "I'm done. I'd just like the check, please."

Azaroth held up a quick hand. "I would like some coffee if you don't mind. Black. And I would like it as hot as…well, as hot as you can possibly make it. That would be lovely."

"Of course," the waitress agreed. "I just put a fresh pot on. I'll have that for you in a minute or two."

Azaroth watched her wander off to another table to check on some other customers, then turned back towards Robert.

"I am not buying your soul, Robert," he assured the man. "That is the beauty of this entire proposal. I am simply going to give you the money. One million dollars, to be specific. Tax free. I will see to it that it is deposited into your bank account in the next half hour. In return, you will owe me…absolutely nothing."

"Bullshit!" Robert barked. "Nothing is free. Especially not coming from you."

Azaroth laid a hand on the table, palm down. When he raised it back up, there was a large gold coin laying on the polished wooden surface. A silhouetted demon was emblazoned on the upward face of the coin, complete with horns, pointed tail, and pitchfork. Azaroth picked up the coin and held it between the thumb and forefinger of his right hand. He held it at eye level to allow Robert to examine it more closely, then turned it to reveal a simple pentagram etched into the reverse side.

"The money is yours, and you owe me nothing," he repeated. "In addition to the one million, I will give you this gold coin. Should you ever run out of cash, you need only hold up the coin and say 'I want more'. I will happily provide you with whatever additional sum you desire. Name it and it is yours. However, this second payment will no longer be a gift. You will have to provide me with something in return."

"My soul," Robert muttered.

"Yes. That would be the agreement. And, of course, you would also need to return my coin. One transaction per customer. I am sure you understand."

Robert nodded, staring at his empty plate and contemplating the arrangement. After a long silence, he peered up at Azaroth. "If I never ask for any more money?"

"Then I get nothing. Your soul is your own, and I will never bother you again. As I said, the money I give you today is a gift. No cost and no strings."

Azaroth flipped the coin towards Robert. Startled, Robert threw out his hands to catch it, but the coin flared a brilliant white and disappeared in mid-air, making a popping noise as it winked out of existence. The demon held out his left fist and opened the hand to reveal the coin now resting in his palm.

"Do we have a deal?" he asked.

"A million dollars, and all I have to do is never ask for any more?"

"Yes, Robert." There was a slight edge to Azaroth's voice now. "I thought I made that clear. Do…we…have…a…deal?"

Robert paused a moment longer before answering. Tentatively, he held out his hand, palm up.

"Yes, I accept."

Azaroth laid the coin in Robert's outstretched hand, the demon silhouette facing up. As soon as he released it, the demon image on the coin twitched its tail and waved its tiny pitchfork at Robert. In revulsion, Robert recoiled, dropping the coin onto the table where it bounced once and began to roll. The gold disk travelled along the length of the lacquered surface, fell off the edge of the table, and disappeared again with another tiny pop of air.

"See? That is the beauty of the gold coin," Azaroth said with a light chuckle. "You cannot lose it. Check your shirt pocket."

Robert patted his chest and felt a heavy weight under his hand. He reached into his pocket and removed the coin. This time, to the man's relief, the demon remained motionless. Not wanting to hold on to the object any longer than he absolutely had to, Robert dropped it back into his pocket.

"It will always be with you," Azaroth continued. "You cannot lose it, spend it, or give it away. This assures you will never lose the opportunity to ask for more money if you need it simply because you carelessly misplaced your coin. Is that not convenient?"

Robert nodded but did not answer.

The waitress returned, set a steaming white mug down in front of Azaroth, and laid the bill on the table between him and Robert.

"Is there anything else I can bring either of you?" she

asked.

Azaroth shook his head, thanked her politely, and sent her on her way. He laid a hand over the bill and pulled it towards him.

"I will cover the check. Another little gift. No strings. Now, perhaps you would like to head on over to your bank and check your current balance? Maybe make a small withdrawal? You could pay your rent and then take yourself on a bit of a shopping spree. You could probably do with some new clothes, if what you are wearing today is any indication."

Robert said nothing. He slid out of the booth and rose quickly.

"I will see you later," Azaroth told him. "Or not. Completely your decision, of course."

Robert nodded one more time, a fast duck of the head, then hastily retreated from the restaurant.

Azaroth watched him go, listening to the smack of the small silver bell affixed to the door frame as Robert exited the business. He smiled, though the expression was far from friendly. The sharp-toothed grin perfectly matched the predatory gleam in Azaroth's eyes.

He would see this human again. He was certain of that. The demon had carefully vetted his target, and he was confident the man would not be content with the paltry sum he had just received. He would want more. Azaroth had got quite adept at judging the souls that wandered this world, and the gold coin was proof of that.

He had been using that very same coin for over three hundred years, and during that time, it had always been willingly handed back to him.

Azaroth took a sip of the coffee. It was indeed hot. The dark liquid scalded his lips, tongue, and throat on the way down. He sighed in contentment, then emptied the mug in one long swallow.

True Intentions

by Gabriella Balcom

Thumbing through the last bundle of money, Giles smiled, then put it with the others in his sock drawer. He'd cashed the newest cheques today. Adding the latest $42,450 now brought the grand total to $345,870. He'd been promised $12,000 more in two days but didn't plan to collect it; he already had enough.

"Giles, you're a genius," he said, eyeing his reflection in the mirror over the dresser. Then he smirked.

Last year, several tornadoes had hit Texas, leaving trails of devastation in their wake. Forming a "Rebuild Ravaged Homes" campaign, Giles had spoken of his desire to help the victims who'd lost their homes. He'd asked for investments rather than contributions and promised that each dollar people invested would be returned to them doubled, courtesy of generous, wealthy backers who'd already given their commitments. So many individuals had delved deeply into their pockets, including a good number of those personally affected by the tornadoes.

None of them knew the full scope of Giles' plans or

his true intentions.

Smiling, he imagined himself on a tropical island somewhere—sandy beaches; clear, sparkling water; brilliant sun overhead; and long, lazy days filled with intoxicating drinks, the best food, massages, and women. Plenty of women. All these things and more were his for the taking and he couldn't wait.

However, when he turned away from his dresser, he flinched to see a woman standing only a few feet away, watching him. "Who are you?" he demanded.

"I've been called many names, including Justice," she replied. "Also Vengeance. But you may call me Ria." She glanced past him at the now closed drawer. "You have a lot of money."

Giles studied the woman—from the long, ebony hair cascading down her back to the white robe covering her slim figure, to the tips of her red, high-heeled boots. He guessed she was in her mid-twenties. "My doors were locked, so how did you get in?" he finally asked. Although his voice was calm and only mildly curious, he felt his anger rising.

"Easily," Ria replied. "Did you win the lottery?"

"In a manner of speaking. Now—what are you doing here?"

"People trusted you. Many of them gave you their

entire life savings. And you don't even care."

Giles narrowed his eyes. "How do you know—?"

"That you're a cold-blooded swindler?" she interrupted. "I know everything. Discerning the truth is one of my gifts."

He snorted, "I'll tell you some truth." Walking towards her, he grabbed her neck with both hands and squeezed as hard as he could. "I'm not interested in anything you have to say, and I couldn't care less what stupid name you call yourself. You shouldn't have come here, and I can't let you leave. Not knowing what you do."

Ria didn't respond in the way he'd expected. Instead of crying out and struggling to get free—or even dying— she laughed and brushed his hands aside as if they were nothing. "You'd commit murder with the same lack of remorse you felt while stealing," she stated, then gestured towards his dresser. His sock drawer promptly opened. Stacks of money rose into the air and the bands on them slid off. Hundred-dollar bills separated from their bundles and floated towards him.

Giles' mouth gaped open for a few seconds before he snapped it shut. As the first hundreds neared him, he just stared at them wide-eyed. The first darted forward to lightly slice his cheek. He barked in surprise and pain when another did the same, but cut him deeper. Blood beaded in the wound, then ran down his face.

Dozens of bills swooped towards him, gashing open his skin in turn, and red droplets flew through the air.

Shrieking, Giles threw up his arms to protect his face, but the money flashed around him, targeting the rest of his body and slashing through clothing and skin alike. Blood soon dripped from his arms, stomach, and legs. "Make them stop," he begged. "I'll return the money."

Expressionless, Ria merely watched. More blood hurtled through the air, some landing on her cloak, some on her cheek. She reached up to dab the moisture with a finger, then tasted it.

Although Giles screamed again and again, the attack didn't stop. His voice had already gone hoarse, and soon, he lost it completely. Blood poured from dozens of deepening wounds.

Eventually, the room stilled again, and the money fluttered to the ground—but only after he lay unmoving on the floor—in a pool of blood.

With a snap of Ria's fingers, the droplets splattered across her robe disappeared. A second snap restored the blood-soaked bills to their original condition, after which they stacked themselves into piles on the dresser.

Ria looked up into the air. One by one, then by the dozens, faces appeared—all those who'd been swindled by Giles. When she nodded, the money vanished, returned to those from whom it had been unrightfully stolen.

Glancing around, Ria surveyed the rivulets of blood all over the room, then smiled. She stepped over the man's lifeless body, opened the door, and went outside.

Don't Mess with the Horses

by Ximena Escobar

They wanted the land for their beef cattle, so they slaughtered the wild horses. Corpses thrown unceremoniously on the burn pile.

Huge flames swelled and the men stood aback, overwhelmed by the burning heat so intense, it grew legs.

Fire horses leapt out of the blaze, galloping after them. Their hellish trail lit the grasslands, consumed the men and their screams—flesh and bone sizzling on the hot ground.

The driver that would transport the beef to the site chewed contentedly on his drumstick, grateful for the day off. The weather looked great, and he could already smell a barbecue.

The End Credits

by Galina Trefil

"I love you, Stan," she told him, looking up from the TV screen to where he sat opposite her in a lazy boy. His scowl made clear that her efforts were useless. She hadn't given in to his earlier request and he was still stewing. "I love you," she repeated, this time louder, but his glare only deepened. She sighed, shaking her head back and forth. Showing Stan affection, either in word or action, was always like pouring water into a cup that had, had a holed drilled into its base. There was no sating him. Like a baby mockingbird, he always wanted more, more, *more*. "My dear, must you be so sour? Why, this is your favourite show and you haven't laughed a single time. The program's almost over. Can't you try to smile?"

"Why should I?"

"So that we can enjoy our evening together."

"You think that I can enjoy my time with you?"

"I would like you to, yes. I certainly do enjoy it when you come to visit."

"It's easy to say that," he snapped, "but words are cheap."

Ah, yes, she sighed. Here it comes again. Her boy had always had a terrible temper, but this particular issue, more than others, always set him off.

"You're so damn stingy," he began. "You're always acting like I won't pay you back. Don't you care how that makes me feel? I mean, you're demeaning me!"

"Oh, Stanley, that's not my intention."

"Don't pretend that you don't know exactly what you're doing. You act like you're not getting off on it, but withholding aid really does it for you. Admit it. You're just thrilled to watch me have to grovel."

"No, Stanley, that's not it. It's just that I want you to do well *for yourself*. You're a grown man, not a child. It's not good for you to keep coming to me for help…

At some point, you've got to take responsibility for your own bills."

He scowled, his lower lip protruding. "If you really loved me, like you say, you'd trust me."

"I do trust you, honey. It's just that I'm old and I have to be careful with my savings." He huffed, folding his arms over his chest tightly. "Someday, I'm going to have to go into a nursing home. Stanley, I'm seventy-eight years old. I can't make it on my own forever."

"But I'm your son—your only son. You're supposed to take care of me, Ma. That's a law of nature."

"You have to take some responsibility for your actions. Get a job. I know you've had a rough patch, but there's a lot of opportunities out there…"

"This isn't about me having a job. I came to you for help. I humiliated myself, just like you like me to do. I did everything but get down on my knees and still, you won't part with a nickel."

She felt herself deflating like an old, withered balloon. She pushed herself up and made her way into the kitchen. As she sat at the table with her cheque book, she let out a long sigh. She wasn't sure who she was more disappointed with—him, for badgering her for the umpteenth time for cash, or herself, for giving in, like they both knew she always would.

Stanley always spoke to her as though she had utter contempt for him. But she didn't. She loved her boy—always had. Perhaps she had loved him too much, which was why he was still, even in his fifties, sucking at her financial teat. When he had been born, oh, what hopes she'd had for him—what aspirations! At some point, she'd acknowledged that all of them were unrealistic though. He was a born loser—a pathetic failure, just as his father had been.

And these days, money was the one and only way to make him be civil. She stared at the cheque for a long time. How coarse and derisive it felt beneath her fingertips…and yet she tore it out of the book and, frustrated, made her way back into the living room, where Stanley was still glaring at the TV. "Here," she remarked, capitulating as much defeat as she was willing to. His countenance brightened as his stubby fingers snatched it away. "Now we can at least watch the last ten minutes of *Perfect Strangers* in peace," she grumbled, sitting back on the couch.

"Ma, this is only for $500. My rent's $1000."

"I've been telling you for a long time that you need to move to a less expensive apartment."

"What are you talking about? Do you think this is still the 1950s? There are no less expensive apartments anymore," he protested. "I live in a dump as it is."

"A two-bedroom dump. You don't need all that extra space."

"Well, that doesn't matter right now because I need $500 more. You have to write me another cheque."

"No."

"No?"

"I won't do it, lambchop. This is all that I can part with. If you would take care of me, this wouldn't be an issue. But every time that I get sick, you're never here for me. I know, if I am ever in a bad enough situation, a retirement home is going to be my only option. That means I have to save up."

"Oh, knock it off. We both know that you'll never go into one of those hellholes. You're always threatening to, but if you were going to go, you'd have done it a long time ago." Her lower lip quivered. "How much do you have stored at this point anyway? Ten thousand? Twenty thousand? Hell, I wouldn't be surprised if it's a lot more…" Her eyes flicked over in his direction briefly, but she didn't respond. "It *is* a lot more, isn't it?" he inquired, his tone growing low and hungry. "Just how much? How much is it, Ma? Damn it, tell me!"

"How much I have in savings is not your concern."

"Like Hell, it isn't! You're leaving it to me, aren't you?"

"Yes, Stanley. Everything that I have, I'm leaving to you."

"Then why won't you tell me how much it is?"

"Because I don't know how much will still be left over once I go into a home. I could be there for years, sweetheart. My pension won't be enough to cover it."

"And what happens to me then?"

She picked up a teacup sitting on the coffee table between them. Its contents were cold and unfulfilling as they trickled down her throat. "You will just have to make your own way then. You'll have to do it without me, honey—which is why you need to buckle down now and learn to finally, at last make your own way. I won't be here for you forever."

"I can make it without you just fine!" he scoffed. "You always talk like you've made life easier for me. Being your son was the hardest damn thing in the world. Other people think you're a saint, but they have no idea of how manipulative and cruel you really are."

Her eyes brimmed with tears, but she was quiet as he continued his lengthy tirade. Usually, the $500 would've bought a few minutes of peace with him, but not today. On and on and on he went, with each word slamming into her heart like an ice pick.

Why was he like this? She could accept that he hadn't got married or given her grandchildren. She could ignore that he'd always railed against authority figures, which had resulted in him never being employed for more than a few months at a time. She was aware that he wasn't very bright or even good looking. But…couldn't he at least have been kind? Was it too much to ask that he have just been a devoted son? Did he have to be so damn greedy?

"You've got a lot of nerve, talking about nursing homes." She blinked, coming out of her dissociative stupor. "Yeah, that's right. You heard me," Stanley grumbled. "I mean, I'm not inheriting anything from Pop. You're the only one who's going to leave me jack. And you keep talking about nursing homes when you know they'll leave your bank account bone dry! Don't you have any shame?"

"What do you mean? Are you saying that you'd take care of me? Move in here with me and do all the cooking and cleaning?"

He snorted.

"Well, then," she snapped, "what alternative to a rest home do I have?"

"Oh, I can think of one. I shouldn't have to say it."

She knit her eyebrows, shocked. "I…I think that you are going to have to say it, my dear. Go on. Now's not the time to be quiet, darling. Get it off your chest!"

"All that I'm saying, Ma…is that it's been hard to be your son. You've made it hard. I deserve compensation. Whatever you have to do to make sure that I have it…well…sometimes extreme measures are called for."

"You want me to kill myself? Stanley," she choked, "am I understanding you correctly? You'd rather I kill myself than spend the money having professionals take care of me?"

"Don't sound so dramatic. It's not like you'd be special. Lots of people kill themselves. And, at your age, it's not like you're losing that much. Hell, you're only one fall away from being in a walker. You're in dentures. You haven't had a date in twenty years. Your version of an exciting time is going to the salon to get your hair done. Half of your friends are dead. You don't even have a cat to take care of. Face it, Ma: yours is a pathetic existence. The world won't miss you. If you bit the bullet now, literally speaking, the only difference that it makes is that it'd prevent those leeches at the home from getting what you should, by all means, want to go to your own flesh and blood."

She blinked, a degree of shock setting in. Always, she told herself how much she loved him. But right now…right now, she couldn't even stand to look at him. "I'll just…I'll just go make out another cheque," she whispered, staring at the screen as the end credits began to roll.

A few minutes later, she returned, hand trembling, as she held the second slip of paper out to him. "$63,472.83!" Stanley jumped up with a shriek, cradling the cheque against his chest like a new-born baby. "Ma, I can't believe you're actually—"

Boom. His eyes went wide and then dropped down towards his belly, to the spreading red stain on his shirt there.

She was a good shot, but even if she wasn't, she was certainly close enough to shoot him where he would've died instantly. She chose not to. "If it is only my money that you care about, my dear, then I give it to you—every cent. And not one of those cents will go to the home. But I will still need to be provided for, Stanley… If you won't care for me, I suppose that prison will."

As he dropped to his knees, she fixed her gaze on the opening of the next sitcom. "I always liked this show," she murmured absently, taking another sad swig of frigid tea. As he began to crawl towards the phone, she gave little thought to whether or not the hospital would be able to save him. Either way, to her, he was already gone.

Farming

by Raven Corinn Carluk

Tim closed the door to his server farm with a sigh. The crisp scents of ozone and air conditioner were replaced immediately by must and damp. His mum's house never smelled clean, but there wasn't much he could do about it—other than simply tolerate the problem while farming for coins.

Free room and board didn't come without a price.

He made his way up the creaky stairs, checking the newsfeed with his Implant. Headlines scrolled at the bottom of his field of vision, bright against the dinginess of the basement. Nothing important happening in the world—just more fights, more company closures, more poverty, more crime. Even if they *were* important issues, what could a simple Bitcoin farmer do about them?

Tim stepped into the brightly lit hall and immediately squinted. "Mum, is breakfast ready?" He'd been up all night tweaking the algorithms, and the thirty-year-old man craved Mum's bacon and eggs.

A whimper came from the kitchen.

He scurried down the hall, frowning sharply. Had

Mum fallen and was bleeding out on the linoleum floor? She could have been there for hours while he worked on his servers. What was he supposed to do? Would emergency services get here in time?

Tim burst into the kitchen, then slid to a stop, staring at the scene before him.

His mother was duct-taped to one of the dinette chairs, a tea towel shoved in her mouth. Tears streamed down her cheeks, and one eye had started to swell shut. She called out when she saw him, though it was too muffled to make out the words.

Around her stood three men in dark clothes and balaclavas. Tall and thin, they were still bigger than Tim, all three fidgeting with nervous energy, knives sheathed at their hips.

"I was beginning to think we'd have to come get you." Laughed the masked man directly beside his Mum. He laid a hand on her shoulder. "Guess we shoulda let her finish making breakfast."

Tim spun, heart racing. He needed to get to his server farm; it doubled as a panic room. He could ring the cops from there, let the professionals handle the intruders.

A fourth man blocked his path. Laughing, the newcomer grabbed Tim by the upper arms and marched him to the kitchen table.

"Oh, man, the look on your face." Uno, as Tim thought of him, laughed, clapping Mum on the shoulder. Dos and Tres chuckled, moving closer to each other, and Quatro squeezed Tim's shoulders. "Really shoulda brought a camera."

"What do you want?" Tim squeaked out. Cold sweat beaded his skin, and he struggled to breathe.

Uno shook his head. "You're the richest Bitcoiner in the city, and you *really* have to ask?" He drew his knife. "I'd heard you were pretty smart."

Tim swallowed hard and activated his personal firewall. They wouldn't be able to hack his Implant to get his password and wallet ID. He'd earned the millions of coins, and there was no way he was going to let random creeps steal from him.

"So this is how it's gonna go." Uno stroked Mum's hair with the knife blade. "You're gonna transfer four million coins into our wallet, or I'm gonna start carving pieces off your Mum here." She started crying anew.

He shook his head, eyes wide, mouth moving but no words coming out. Of course, he'd been attacked online: hackers trying to breach his password, scammers trying to phish his details. But he'd never been physically assaulted, never had to see the eyes of someone with a weapon. This was more than he knew how to handle.

Uno pressed the blade hard under her chin, and Mum screamed through her gag.

"No!" Tim shouted, pressing back in his chair. Quatro clamped down harder on his shoulders, but the coin farmer wasn't trying to escape. "You can't have my money."

Uno tipped his head. "Perhaps you don't understand what's gonna happen." He snapped his fingers, and Dos dropped to his knees in front of Mum, pulling his knife. Tim said nothing, and Dos sliced Mum's calf.

Even the towel couldn't muffle her shriek of pain.

Tim shook his head, biting his lip. Mum squirmed against the tape, Uno keeping the knife lightly against her throat. Dos clutched Mum's ankle while glaring at Tim, knife at the ready, blood staining his hand. "The transfer?"

He shook his head again. "No. I can't." Tim swallowed, looking down. "I won't."

Dos drove the blade into Mum's foot with a grunt. She screamed and squirmed, tears pouring from clenched eyes. Dos pulled the knife free, then stabbed her other foot. A crunching wet noise sounded louder than Mum's shrieks, something he'd never heard, even in movies. Too real, too visceral, too unbelievable.

Tim swallowed down a wave of bile as the scent of blood assaulted him. Mum's broken sobbing filled the kitchen, and the robbers silently watched, waiting for Tim to break.

He wouldn't give them anything. It was *his* coin. If they wanted to have as much as he did, *they* could install the hardware, maintain the servers, and tweak their own algorithms. Tim refused to give in, even as Mum's cries grew weaker and the blood scent grew stronger.

Uno swore. "I *will* do it." Tim glanced up. Uno had pulled Mum's head back, the knife tight against her taut throat. When Tim shook his head, Uno performed the killing slice.

Tim cried out. He pulled against Quatro's grip. He sobbed. He swore at them. He watched Mum's eyes lose their light, her life surging down her housecoat.

"Pull his Implant. Try to get the password."

"What if we can't brute-force it?" Tres asked, approaching the slender coin farmer.

"Trash the servers. No one gets it." The robbers laughed, surrounding Tim. His blood ran cold, but all he could do was watch them carve his Implant free of his skull. Pain slowly faded as he slumped next to his mother's already cooling corpse.

The Influencer

by Jacqueline Moran Meyer

The winged gargoyle perched at the end of the stone ledge waits for me, as it stares down at southern Manhattan. The sun will set in about an hour, and the sky has exploded in colour. Taking in the width and length of the ledge which extends from the rooftop, I peer over the stone at the thirty-five-floor pre-war building's brick facade. My stomach lurches while I try to digest the dizzying distance from here to the asphalt below.

My social media influencer status took a beating last year. I suffered a severe fall from grace and lost everything: my followers, my sponsors, my reputation, and, worst of all, my money. My mom suggested getting a "real" job, which made me only more determined to get my following back. I visited a for-real psychic, Lady Claire V Yont. She told me one of my haters must have placed a strong curse of failure on me. To break this curse and have my next photo go viral, with more likes than I have ever received on any posts combined, she said I needed to face a fear. Lady Yont suggested I post a photo on my account of me doing something that pushes all my fear buttons. It's no secret to my friends and family that I am deathly afraid of heights.

My objective is to traverse the approximately fifteen-foot-long, three-foot-wide ledge out to the gargoyle. Once there, I'll put on the stilettos I am being paid to model. Graham will take a few photos. I'll go back home and post them online. I only need one killer photo. Easy.

"This will be a hot post, babe," says Graham, my boyfriend of three years.

"Uh-huh," I say. My body is shaking, and I am finding it hard to form real words.

"Sick, right? I told you it would be good," Graham says, hovering over me. A smile spreads on his unnaturally handsome face. His tanned skin and blond hair come from bottles and his blue eyes from contacts. He looks like he belongs on a beach, but he is a New York City boy, through and through.

"This post will be a money maker, I'm sure," Graham says.

I step out of my flip-flops and adjust the cups of my white macramé bikini top, which barely covers my newly acquired breasts. Graham hands me the high heels. I'm being paid five thousand dollars for five posts. At the height of my success, I earned thirty thousand dollars per post, but money is money, and this is a new start.

"I'm ready."

I bite my lip while I let Graham lift me and plant my butt on the mantel.

"I'm freezing." The stone feels like a block of ice against my ass, my thong bikini bottom doing nothing to protect my skin.

My boyfriend pouts.

"Go slow. Don't look down," Graham says.

Like a child told not to touch a hot stove before burning their fingers, I, of course, turn my head behind me and glance down—despite the cold, sweat forms on my upper lip. I hesitate, trying to talk myself out of this stunt, but I'm desperate for cash. The more treacherous the shot, the more likes I will generate; increased likes mean more followers, and more followers make me more attractive to sponsors.

"Do I look ok?"

Graham has a lot invested in my comeback. He's an aspiring influencer also, and my arrest on those lame fraud charges affected his wallet, too. Our relationship is tenuous, dangling by a thread.

"You're hot. You're not called the Kim twin for no reason."

"Don't take any photos until I'm settled out there," I say. Graham nods.

I breathe in the crisp late summer air. It's starting to feel like fall. I curl up my legs, so my whole body is on the ledge, and stand. I stand, balancing with my arms out to each side, looking straight ahead at the gargoyle's back, his hard-grey wings ready for flight. The ledge appeared wider from the view on the roof. I become hyper aware of my size and weight.

The world opens up on both sides of me; the expanse of the dramatic sky and the tall buildings below makes me swoon. The familiar city sounds of buses and truck engines and the occasional car horn blasts seem miles below me. Goosebumps prickle my skin. "Doin' great babe! Love the view from here," Graham says, laughing. The suddenness of his voice jolts me out of my concentration. I stop and crouch down, my knees and hands on the stone. Hanging my head, I close my eyes, trying to steady myself.

"Shit! Don't do that!" I scream.

"Sorry, Bree," he says under his breath. He doesn't sound the least bit sorry.

"Shhh!" I hiss.

The breeze picks up—a gust of cold wind blows my hair across my face, obscuring my vision. I wish I had tied it back and regretted spending the whole morning under a blow dryer and curling iron.

I pick up my head and stare at the jewel-encrusted shoes. Fake jewels. Vegan leather. I'm all for saving the animals, though—at least online. People like save-the-world garbage, but these heels are fugly. You would not catch me dead wearing these in real life, but I will promote the crap out of them. The ledge is made of stone and will carry my weight. I've convinced myself the reward will be worth the risk. Influencers are constantly doing dangerous shoots.

Moving at the slowest pace possible, focusing on my breathing, I reach the statue and grab one of the gargoyle's wings. I turn and sit, facing Graham with my back leaning against the monster, in between its two outstretched wings. I consider Graham, arms folded, staring up at the sky, presumably worrying about the light's quality.

"You may speak now," I yell.

"Whoo-hoo! Still a nice view, by the way," Graham yells. His booming voice annoys me. "Put the shoes on, and I'll take pics."

"My fingers are frozen! Are my lips blue?"

"That's why God created Photoshop," Graham says. "You're back, baby. Ka-ching, ka-ching."

With quivering numb hands, I start putting on the shoes. I stop several times, resting my head against the gargoyle. My new stone friend almost feels alive—still warm from the heat of the sun beating down on him all day.

My client's competitors accused me of being rewarded with cash to diss them in my vlog posts. I admit, I did receive payment to ruin them, but this is America—free speech is legal. The complaining companies sued me, but that event isn't why my sponsors fired me. My likes, followers, and sponsorship all increased after the lawsuit became top news—after all, any press is good press.

I became a household name among people my age.

The stress of the lawsuit, which I won, took its toll on me. I couldn't eat, and as a result, my weight plunged. Usually, this would be a positive thing online, but I didn't have any weight to lose to begin with. When a bunch of insensitive haters said I looked like a cancer patient, my anger at their rudeness caused me to act impulsively. I clapped back, "I do have cancer."

Once the toothpaste is out of the tube, as my mom always used to say, you can't get it back in. Once I'd lied about having a fatal disease, I couldn't turn back the clock. The sympathy I received made the Money God appear and he opened his golden gates of heaven to me. People started GoFundMe pages for me and would send me the money.

I received endorsement deals for anti-inflammatory

diets, and everyone went through my fraudulent illness journey and miraculous recovery with me. Yes, I lied, but social media is entertainment not reality. My colleagues lie. The Vegan Vlogger dines at Jerry's Steakhouse, chows down on steaks, and laughs about how her followers do not know she cannot live without eating cow. The actor promoting the cheap phone—he has never used it and is posting from his expensive smartphone. Anyway, someone ratted me out, and I blame them for my downfall.

Any press is good press…unless you get caught lying about having cancer.

And that's why this photo needs to shock.

I finish putting the stilettos on, and my hair stands up on end as one foot slips, and dangles over the edge.

"Almost ready," I say to Graham, whose mouth is twisted into a grimace. He has zero patience.

"Tell me when," he huffs.

"Did you just sigh?" I'm annoyed. Graham ignores my question.

I shiver, pinching my cheeks and slapping my arms and legs to warm my skin.

"Is my makeup ok?"

"Fine. Ready?" His impatience is thick. *I would like to see you try to crawl out here, sweetie.*

"One sec," I say, stalling. To irritate him, I take my lip gloss out of the band of my thong and apply some.

"Ready. I'll sit first." I sit back and pose seductively, mouth parted, legs extended, shoulders back.

Graham slides his cell phone out of the back pocket of his surfer shorts. He stretches his arms, holding the phone in front of him, smiling at me.

"Ok. Tilt your head back. Think sexy thoughts."

I close my eyes, tilt my head up to the sky, and smile.

"Fuck," Graham mutters.

I gape over at him through one opened eye.

"Um, Bree… My phone's dead."

"What the hell, Graham! You find out now?!"

"Where's yours?" He glances around.

The only possession I left behind before crawling out here were my sandals.

My body convulses in anger.

"Your apartment!" I shoot the words at him like daggers. Graham used to be so attentive, forgetting to charge his phone would never have happened a year ago when I was a social media phenom. In public, he fawns all over me, but when we are alone, he is always preoccupied.

"Do you want to come back?" he asks, sheepishly.

"No! Are you kidding me? I am never climbing out

on a ledge like this ever again. *Ever!*" I flail my arms and quickly realise how dangerous a movement this is at the moment.

"Calm down. Calm down," Graham says in a hushed voice. His hands move up and down to quiet me.

"Get my goddamn phone! It's getting dark."

"I'll hurry," he says. Graham turns, opens the door leading to the stairwell, and disappears, the metal door closing with a loud clang behind him.

I am alone.

I am alone, sitting on a ledge thirty-five storeys high, freezing, wearing a white thong bikini and ridiculous plastic-jewelled heels, all for one photo. One. Photo. Despite my fear of heights, my eyes peer downwards ay the ant-sized people skittering about below.

Where is he?

I didn't plan on becoming an influencer. My career took off by surprise. After graduating from high school three years ago, I went on a vacation with friends. I spent three years scooping ice cream after school to save enough money for the trip. I have always loved fashion. I'm attractive and creative, so I'm the perfect kind of person for my career.

One photo made my social media account take off. I swam with sharks, and my picture getting bitten on the foot went viral. The shark was a baby, but I wear my small scar like a badge of honour. In the beginning, I had a lot of fun in this new world, before my particular platform became glutted with other people wanting to be like me. I began spending my entire day thinking of ways to generate likes and build my brand.

What I do for a living not only brings in a lot of cash but also provides a service.

I help people.

The average person in their cheap clothes, sitting in their small, dingy apartment, can live vicariously through me.

I provide the gifts of glamour and excitement.

By the end of that first summer, I had gained many followers and started getting sponsorship deals. By the following year, I had over two million followers and many sponsorship deals, I became a millionaire many times over.

Yes, my life changed. I didn't find time for family and friends, most of whom were jealous or became hangers-on—asking to borrow money or begging to be in photos. My parents were unhappy with my instant success. They told me I would sell my soul for a pair of

Gucci sunglasses, and I proudly told them I would. My life became about getting the perfect shot. Then I would edit, post, and wait for the photo to go viral. I won't apologise for my success. My job isn't easy. People can be vicious online. Followers don't think of me as a human being with feelings. I am continuously bashed for my appearance.

Your tits are non-existent.

You're so fake.

Ruff. You're a dog.

Your voice sounds like a dying cat.

I had to develop a Teflon skin and focus on the money.

I stare at the closed metal door, willing Graham to appear.

The sky grows darker and the shadows become grim. Shaking uncontrollably due to the cold, I close my eyes. A tiny drop of water lands on my thigh. I open my eyes and turn them upwards—the sky is cloudy, but there was no forecast for rain today.

A speck of water lands on my arm, then another droplet falls on my shoulder before the heavens open up.

The stone ledge beneath my body becomes increasingly slick as the rain falls—it drips down my face, making it difficult to see. One of my hands slips, and I hear the sickening simultaneous thud and crack of my elbow hitting the ledge. The pain is shocking.

I realise then how easy it is to die.

Grasping one of the gargoyle's wings for support, I debate whether I should stay put and wait for Graham or claw my way back to the roof's safety before the ledge gets too slippery to cross. In every action movie I have ever seen, those who stand still always die—I decide to move, determined to dump Graham's ass at the first opportunity.

I tear the shoes from my feet, but when I try to wrap them around my wrist, my butt slides out from beneath me. The stilettos slip from my hands, gracefully tumbling—almost dancing with each other—and silently float out of sight. I can't see the ground due to the rain and encroaching darkness—I'm glad for small mercies.

I begin to crawl, dragging my knees to create more traction, ignoring the discomfort and agony of my tearing skin. At least I am on the ledge. The seconds present like hours—every moment I fear I will make the wrong move and my short life will be over. My dizziness turns into full-fledged vertigo, and I stare straight down at the stone beneath me, trying to pretend I am crawling across my patio. I don't need a lot of room, but on my patio I wouldn't worry about my deck being slick, nor about crashing to the ground from a great height only to splatter on the street below.

Will I fall on a car? A windshield? A person? Will I take someone out with me? Social media would break if I killed someone.

I make slow progress.

I am halfway back, my knees and hands have become numb, useless tools, unable to keep me upright on the slippery ledge. I lie down—my arms and legs splayed out, spread-eagle, grasping at the corners of the shelf, searching for a life-saving groove or rim to hold on to. Several fingernails tear off with my frantic scratching.

My vision continues to blur as my tears mix with the rain, but I find something to grab on to with all the strength I can muster. I will myself to move again, making the tiniest movements to propel myself forward.

The rain stops. The ledge is still slick, but I believe I have more traction when I'm in motion. The tension in my shoulders is immense, and pain radiates down my arms. Only two more feet and I will be safe. Every bit of agony will have been worth it if I can reach the safety of the rooftop.

The door opens, and Graham's gleaming smile instantly fades when he takes in the sight of me hugging the stone, frantically trying to hold on.

His sudden appearance startles me. I lie down, my face pressed to the ledge, grasping the stone with my hands and feet.

"Help me," I murmur.

Graham doesn't answer, so I lift my head.

My heart sinks. I think I may vomit.

Rather than helping me, Graham is pointing my cell phone at me, taking pictures or a video of my suffering.

"Help," I plead.

Graham comes to his senses and moves in my direction, leaning his body towards me, arms outstretched. One hand reaches for mine, while the other clutches my phone.

I inhale and unclench one hand from the ledge to snatch Graham's.

We make contact and I pull.

I pull with all my remaining strength.

And then he's falling…falling through the air, arms and legs flailing like an insect on its back.

Time alternates between speeding up, slowing down, and standing still. I am hyper aware of his imminent impact.

I am capturing Graham's plummet on film having grabbed my phone from the rooftop where he dropped it before disappearing over the ledge. I'll post it on my social media account and become rich and famous again, getting the most likes on record because of his death.

The gargoyle stares, its expression looks like one of pity from this angle.

I am angry at the thought of it pitying me.

Silver

by Erik Handy

The rain had stopped, and the children were huddled together under their quilt. The floor was hard—the pallet of spare quilts didn't help, but that didn't keep the boy and girl from sleeping. They were grateful for four walls, a roof, and a fire.

Mama stayed up, fixing the holes in her son's pants. One more patch and then she'd join them on the floor. Her eyes were tired and they burned. The only light was the fire on the other side of her children. Flickering orange light cascaded along each inch of the one-room cabin. Still, she needed better light, but there wouldn't be any until dawn. She hoped to finish her chore well before then so she could be ready to work on the next day's tasks. It was truly never ending, but if it did end, then what? What else was there to do in life?

A step on the front porch.

Wood cracking.

Not from a boot heel.

From something…sharper.

A light knock on the door.

Then, a woman's voice.

"Sir," said a meek British accent. "Sir?"

Mama kept the shotgun close at hand ever since Papa went away in the summer. He made her promise to keep it loaded and near. If war hadn't broken out between the states, then he would've been here protecting his family. This fell on Mama, too.

Mama set her boy's pants on the floor.

The children were still asleep.

She slowly picked up the shotgun from behind her chair and went to the door.

"Who is it?" she said, not wanting to wake the children.

"Madame," the visitor said, surprised. "Madame, I apologise for intruding upon you in this late hour."

Mama unlatched the door and let it swing open on its own.

There was a woman in white—that is, if her dress wasn't wet and muddy all around the bottom. Her hair was a matted mess. In drier circumstances, she would have indeed been mighty beautiful. Now, she appeared pathetic, like a neglected hound.

"My name is Ophelia Sherman," she said. "I'm an actress. I was on my way to Dodge when my stagecoach got bogged down in some mud. The driver went on ahead to get some help. That could take hours. I am embarrassed to ask at this ungodly hour, but may I sit by your fire and warm my bones? Just long enough for me to regain my energy?" She saw Mama's shotgun. "I can pay you."

"No need for that," Mama said. "All I ask is you keep your voice down."

Ophelia spotted the sleeping children. "Of course, Madame. I wouldn't dare rile your children and cause you dismay. You need your relief."

"Come in."

Ophelia went to the meagre dining table and gently pulled out a chair.

"Can I offer you some coffee?" Mama said. "I have leftover stew as well."

"No, thank you. Just a seat in a warm home. For a few minutes."

"Stay as long as you like, Miss Sherman."

Ophelia blushed. "And your name, Madame?"

Mama didn't hear her.

The fire…through the woman at her supper table was the fire.

Mama thought it was a trick of the light and her ailing eyes. But the woman's outline stood out against the shimmering translucence contained within her figure. She was solid against the night, but here she was ethereal.

Ignoring the woman—if she was a woman—Mama went back to her chair and the mending.

"If you don't mind," she said, "we can talk while I work. I was nearly finished when you showed up."

"I apologise for interrupting your work."

The woman's sincerity rang true. She was so polite. If only she wasn't see-through…

Mama's head swam with possibilities. They weren't churchgoing folk, but she knew enough to wonder if this was the Devil in the half-flesh, here to take her and her children straight to Hell. Why? Because that was what the Devil did. Evil, for evil's sake.

"Are you all right, Madame?"

Mama squinted at her handiwork. "I don't…mean to stare. That's a…pretty dress."

"This wet, dirty thing? I guess it is."

"You're an actress?"

The woman's smile disarmed Mama. One could imagine its effects on a man's heart.

"I am. Never far from home if there's a stage nearby."

"Dodge does have a theatre. Though I don't know if they'd be receptive to a lady of your calibre."

Ophelia chuckled, then slapped her hand on her mouth. "My apologies, Madame. That is funny. I haven't been called a lady in quite some time."

Mama looked up when she noticed the woman had stopped talking.

Gazing at the fire, Ophelia eventually spoke, "I've been called many names. Names I dare not repeat. But yes—I have been called a lady several times." She smiled again. "Are you certain I cannot repay your hospitality?"

"Nonsense."

"Well, if you and your family make it to Dodge, please see me. I would be delighted to have you as my guests."

Mama returned Ophelia's smile and then returned to the pants she just finished mending. Pretending to work on them gave her time to think. She could not determine what manner of creature sat before her. A devil? A ghost? What other dark things lurked in the cold night?

She cursed herself for not being more educated. Her existence was this home and family. It wasn't much, but caring for them filled her heart as well as the hours of every day. She was raised to believe that was the reason for living. Anything else—money, church, plays—wasn't important. In a perfect world on a perfect night, anything else wouldn't have been important. However, tonight shed new light through the ignored facets of the world.

She wanted to look at the woman again—to prove

her eyesight hadn't deceived her. Would that set her mind at ease?

"Your fire does warm me," Ophelia said. "As does the sight of your children. I'm reminded of, when I was their very age, sleeping on the floor, in a home such as this. My parents did their best, which was more than adequate for a girl like me. They taught me, just as I'm sure you've taught your children, that home is most important—the physical dwelling and the feeling. Does that make sense?"

"It does, Miss Sherman."

"Oh forgive me, Madame. I must be delirious."

"Are you sure you wouldn't like some coffee? I wish we had tea—"

"Thank you, but no. This"—she gestured to the fire—"is all I need at this time. Your children…what are their names?"

"Jacob and Mattie. Eight and six."

"Mere babes. I envy them, their youth. Their…innocence. No. That's not the word I mean. *Inexperience*, perhaps? They can look forward to the rest of their lives." She giggled.

"Indeed," Mama said. "Falling in love. Seeing the world, if they want."

"I've seen a lot of this world. Half this country,

really, and there are good people like yourself and there are bad. But there is so much more."

"Like?"

"Places," Ophelia replied. "Different towns. Different environments. Mountains. Rivers."

"Do you often move around?"

Ophelia's eyes glazed over as she nodded. "Every year, it seems. I don't get bored with each locale. I just want to experience more. It's a hunger I feed. Acting allows me this privilege. There are theatres in just about every town I've visited. And there are patrons willing to pay me to perform." She looked at Mama straight on. "Madame, I will ask again. Please do not take offence. Your kindness and compassion have touched me in a way I did not expect. Do you want money?"

Mama did. That would make her loneliness bearable—to go into town with her head held high while her children wore clothes not twice-patched. It didn't matter to them, but it mattered to her. Living this way gnawed on her self-esteem, especially with her husband on some distant field. She didn't expect money to make her happy, but it could take the chill off her rainy life.

"Please do not be embarrassed," Ophelia said. "I offer you a great amount of money. As you have already surmised, I am more than a mere actress of the stage."

The shotgun was at Mama's feet. It seemed a million miles away.

"There is a tree just beyond your well," Ophelia told her. "Buried at the base of that tree is a sack of silver dollars. You should be able to carry it yourself. If you want it." One more smile and then she stood. "I am warm enough, Madame."

Ophelia Sherman curtsied and let herself out.

Mama sat for a moment.

The door slowly shut.

She reached down, picked up the shotgun, then waited another moment.

The click-clack of heels on the porch was followed by the squishes of trudging through mud.

Mama got up and went to the door, propping it open with her foot.

The woman in white went the way she came, never looking back, fading into the night.

The children slept through the entire encounter. Mama believed their sweet dreams paled in significance to what she just witnessed.

It was deathly quiet. She could gather the shovel from the side of the house and make it to the tree, all while keeping an ear on the children. Her shotgun would be at the ready in case the offer was a trap.

Was the woman a devil? Mama began to wonder if she was an angel.

Or a loon.

Who would make such a claim at this odd hour?

Mama grabbed the lantern but set it back down. She didn't have enough hands to carry that, the shotgun, and a shovel. If her boy was awake, he could've helped. However, she wanted to do this on her own. Her own children might think she was crazy if she went about digging holes in the middle of the night.

She set the shotgun by the door and picked up the lantern. She'd have the shovel in case something more sinister than a bag of silver awaited her. Besides, she watched the woman in white leave, and she didn't hear any strange sounds. Actually, there was absolute silence. The only noise was the shrill ringing in her ears.

She lit the lantern and then set out for the treasure.

She didn't lollygag. Her children were left alone. She would dig for a minute and hope the silver wasn't buried too deep.

Her boots were cold and muddy by the time she reached the tree. She had the site all to herself. She felt like she was in a dream. However, never had a dream thrilled her to this degree. She came in contact with an angel who gifted her a great prize. Kind deeds were usually their own reward, but this time, they truly paid off.

The pull of that money was too great to stop and actually *think* about the situation. Logic was lost. None of this made any sense. Angels. Buried treasure.

Mama planted the shovel into the soft, moist dirt.

From her home came a child's cry.

It was so unexpected and quick that she didn't believe it happened. She couldn't tell whether it was Jacob or Mattie or if it was born from pain or shock.

Silence followed.

After she concluded the scream was a product of her imagination, she stabbed the ground again.

Another scream.

She was sure it was her son.

When she removed the shovel from the earth, the scream stopped.

"It's a test," she said. "God is testing me. If I dig for the silver, my children will yell in pain. I didn't believe in Him before, but I do now."

She dropped the shovel, nearly ashamed for surrendering to greed. She could walk through town with her head held high. All she had to do was not look at the ground.

Another scream.

Her daughter this time.

But she didn't dig…

Mama sprinted across the boggy yard, reaching the porch as one of her children screamed again. The cry was so frantic that she couldn't tell who it came from.

She rushed inside.

There was no more noise from either of her children.

Amid the background of the flickering fireplace, her daughter's body sprawled atop the pile of quilts. The only thing between her head and her neck was a fistful of muscle and bone. There should have been more blood.

Squatting above her was the woman in white, holding the boy with one long hand and yanking his intestines from his small body with the other, shovelling them into her chattering mouth. *Click clack* went her teeth as she chewed.

The shotgun was in pieces, ripped apart like the children.

Mama wished they had stayed asleep.

Getting a Taste

by Chisto Healy

"Now you've gotta kill him," Tony said.

Michael was pacing, rubbing at his scalp. "I don't know, Tony. Killing isn't me, man. I don't kill people."

Tony smacked him in the chest. "You have no choice. He saw your face. The second we leave, he'll go straight to the police. If you go down, we both go down, and I'm not frickin' going down, you hear me? I plan to rob a lot more people after today."

The door was ajar. Michael looked through the small space at the man tied to a chair in the next room. His head hung towards his lap, and he was bleeding from his hairline. Michael shook his head. He grabbed a bottle of whiskey off the counter, unscrewed the cap, and then downed a gulp. He closed his eyes and felt the burn, and the world slowed down. He could breathe and think clearly, steady his heart. When he opened his eyes, he looked at Tony and said, "You want him dead, you kill him."

Tony slapped him in the face. Michael's hand balled into a fist and then relaxed. He took another gulp of whiskey. "It's got to be you," Tony said. "Murder is an extra charge. I'm not catching the extra charge because you screwed up. You screwed up, you fix it. That's how it works."

Michael took a few more swallows of whiskey. He wanted to argue, but Tony had a point. It was his mistake. He leaned down too close, believed the guy, and got his mask ripped off. Crazy bastard grabbed it with his teeth. Michael reacted. He knocked him around pretty good for the trick, but that wasn't really enough, was it? The whole reason he pulled the mask off was for leverage. He knew the danger in seeing their faces. There was no way around killing him.

Michael paced around the kitchen, gulping the whiskey down. He couldn't let Tony clean up his mess, take that charge for him if they got caught. This was his responsibility, but he had never killed anybody before. He didn't even know if he could. He was about to find out, though. He wanted to keep robbing houses with Tony. Taking from people felt good.

"I'm gonna start loading up. Get it done and let's get out of here. When you're adding murder to the breaking and entering and armed robbery, it's not too smart to hang around," Tony told him.

"Yeah. Alright. I'll take care of it," Michael said,

punctuating it with more whiskey. He opened the door and stepped into the walk-in pantry/laundry room. Immediately, the man tied to the chair looked up at him through his one good eye. The other was puffy, purple, and swollen shut. "Don't frigging look at me," Michael said.

He gulped the whiskey. The man kept staring. "I said don't look at me," Michael growled. He could feel the burn of the whiskey, warming his insides. It steeled his nerves. He started looking around the room for a good murder weapon. Tony was the one with a gun, but he never actually loaded it. That was an extra charge too, and Tony was smart. All people had to do was see the gun, and they complied with his demands.

"You don't have to do this," the man said.

"Shut up," Michael told him. He found the toolbox and started looking through it.

"Please. I've got money that isn't in the house. We can go to the bank together and I can get it for you."

"I said shut up." Michael selected a screwdriver. He walked over to the man and he shivered, but he quickly fixed it with a gulp of whiskey. Then he nodded and bounced in place. It was time. He had to get it done. Tony was gonna be angry if he took too long. After another gulp of whiskey, Michael rammed the screwdriver into the man's ear. It went in deep, and he screamed in agony, but when he looked at Michael, he was still very much alive. "Oh, holy crap," Michael said. "That's messed up."

He couldn't bring himself to pull it back out, even with the power of whiskey guiding him. He turned back to the toolbox to find something else before he vomited. It all seemed like crap. Behind the toolbox was a power drill. That had to do it. He took it and plugged it in. Then he looked at the man with his eyes swollen shut and the screwdriver sticking out of the side of his head, and he finished off the bottle, setting it on the washing machine.

He bounced up and down again and then put the drill to the man's forehead. He drilled straight through while the guy screamed. When he stopped, the man was staring at him with wild eyes and a hole clear through his skull. "Damn," Michael snapped. "Killing someone is harder than it sounds."

"Look at me," the man moaned. "He'll think I'm dead. You can go."

"No way. Screw that. I need more alcohol." Michael stormed back to the kitchen and found another bottle of whiskey. He was glad. He didn't want to mix different alcohols. He would throw up for sure then. He fumbled with it until he got it open and then took a few big swallows, which resulted in coughing. He shook it off and then took it with him back into the laundry room. He looked at the guy tied to the chair. He was a damned mess. It was freaking gross. He really needed to find a way to off the sonofabitch. Then he saw something that gave him an idea, and he smiled.

"What are you doing?" the man moaned as Michael started rummaging through the laundry supplies.

Michael took a gulp of whiskey and turned to glare at him. "I told you to shut the hell up. Damn it. Just shut up."

He found what he was looking for and turned around, whiskey in one hand and bleach in the other. He turned the bottle of whiskey up for a few good seconds and then placed it next to the empty one. He was going to need both hands.

Michael walked up to the guy and grabbed his head. He held it back with one hand and poured the bleach into the hole he had made with the drill. The man screamed and screamed, and then he didn't. Steam came from the hole in his head. The smell was strong, and it burned Michael's eyes. He stepped back and saw the blood that had run from the guy's eyes and nose. "Wow. That is seriously messed up," Michael said.

But he did it. The guy was dead, and he did it. He killed somebody. He believed he could probably do it again. He thought it would probably be even easier the next time. He just needed some alcohol, and he could do anything. He picked up the bottle and drank from it.

The door opened. Tony stepped into the room with him. "Did you…"

He didn't finish the sentence. He looked at the guy and turned, puking onto the floor. Michael started laughing. "You think that's funny?" Tony asked as he stood, wiping his mouth. "What the hell is wrong with you?"

"Nothing," Michael said. He grabbed the empty whiskey bottle and slammed it against the washing machine, breaking it. Then he turned with the broken end in his hand and slashed it across Tony's throat. The jagged class cut through but then got caught. Blood was gushing from him like a faucet had been turned on. His eyes were wide with shock. Michael was tugging at the glass, trying to finish the job. It ripped and tore at his open throat but remained stuck. "I actually feel great," Michael said. "Good old liquid courage, am I right?"

Tony fell to his knees and then collapsed face down in the pool of his own blood that gathered on the floor. "Holy crap. That's a lot of blood," Michael said. "But good news…no murder charge for you, brother. Hell, you're getting off scot-free. You should thank me." That was easier, he thought.

Michael laughed and then realised that the wife was tied up upstairs. He smiled excitedly. "Oh hell yeah," he said, taking the bottle and hurrying from the pantry.

He slipped on Tony's blood and skated across the kitchen, slamming into the sink. He laughed his ass off and then turned the bottle up for a few seconds. Then he drunkenly stumbled into the living room and to the staircase where he grabbed the railing to steady himself. He looked back at the blood he had tracked and smeared everywhere, and he laughed again. Then he chugged some whiskey and started up the steps. He made it a third of the way and then fell, laughing as he collided with the staircase.

Then he was up and moving again. He swayed and almost fell again, but made it to the top and grabbed the wall. He stumbled his way to the bedroom where the wife was tied to the bed. When he walked in, she screamed.

"Oh, no!" he said, throwing his hands up with a smile on his face. "I forgot my mask. Looks like I'm gonna have to kill you." He laughed at his own joke.

The woman just kept screaming hysterically. Michael opened the dresser and grabbed a rolled up pair of socks from one of the drawers. Then he stormed over to the bed and stuffed it into her mouth. "Why the hell don't you people ever shut up?" he said.

The second fifth was still half full. He wasn't going to break it and waste alcohol. He had to find something else to kill her with. He stumbled around the room and lost his footing, falling into the vanity against the wall. He shattered the mirror and fell onto the floor. He laid there on his back and took a drink of the whiskey. He chuckled. "This stuff makes it easier to kill, but it makes it hard as hell to walk," he said, laughing.

Michael looked around at all the broken glass. Then he said, "Nah. I used glass already. That's boring."

He grabbed the vanity and tugged himself to his feet. The bottle slipped from his hand, but he caught it and sighed with relief. The woman had managed to spit out the socks. "Where's Larry?" she asked. "Where's my husband? Did you kill him?"

"Where's Larry? Did you kill him?" Michael said, mocking her in an exaggerated voice. He looked at the vanity. The curling iron would be fun, but it would take forever. There was a pair of cuticle scissors, but they were awfully small. He took another gulp of whiskey. "Tell me something good to kill you with," he said, laughing.

The woman just stared at him.

"Oh sure," Michael said. "The one time I actually want to hear from you, you're gonna be freaking quiet."

She still said nothing. He snarled and stumbled to the closet. He almost fell trying to pull it open. "Damn, I'm drunk."

He looked in the closet and started laughing. "Oh hell, that's good," he said. He grabbed something and turned towards her. He was holding a bowling ball. It was a fifteen-pound ball, decorated with a maroon swirl. "This yours or Larry's?" he asked.

"Larry's," she said quietly.

"Looks like raspberry sherbet," he said, carrying it over to the bed. He put the liquor bottle on the nightstand, and he climbed onto the bed, straddling her.

"Please don't," she said.

"Don't what?" Michael asked, holding the bowling ball in two hands over her head.

"Kill me," she said.

"Okay," Michael said. Then he slammed the bowling ball down on her face. He lifted it again, and she was staring up at him with a crushed nose and broken teeth cutting through torn lips.

"What?" Michael laughed. "You said, kill me. I'm just doing what you said." He laughed again and brought the bowling ball back down.

When he lifted it, she coughed blood. Her eye socket was broken. "Holy crap," Michael said. "That's gruesome." He brought the ball down again and again. He lifted it again and saw the eye that wasn't ruined moving back and forth. His mouth fell open in awe. *Human beings are resilient,* he thought. It actually takes a lot of work to kill someone. That was what made it so fun though, he realised. He brought the ball down on her head over and over until there was nothing left to smash. He left the ball on the pillow where her head should have been. He went to climb off the bed and fell. He crawled for a second and then got to his unsteady feet.

He grabbed the bottle off the end table and took a drink. Then he looked at the woman's body and cracked up laughing. "Well, Mrs Bowling Ball Head, my work here is done," he said laughing.

Michael took the bottle with him and left the room. He reached the top of the stairs and lost his footing. He tumbled end over end down the stairs and fell into the blood-stained living room. He groaned in pain and laid there for a moment. Then he looked at his hand and realised he managed to not break the liquor bottle. He laughed and then started cheering. He drank the last of what was in the bottle and then hurled it into the kitchen where it hit the island and shattered.

He laid there for a few minutes until he thought he could stand. Then he walked out the front door into the cool night air. There wasn't a neighbour for a while. Tony picked this house for that reason. Tony was smart. Michael didn't trust himself to drive. He was way too drunk for that. He could wind up killing somebody. He laughed out loud at the thought, knowing there was no one around to hear him. Besides, the car was Tony's anyway.

Michael cut through the woods and walked for an hour until he made it back to town. Only then did he realise that he forgot to take the money and jewellery that Tony had collected. *That's alright,* he thought. He learned tonight that he could take something from people that was a lot more valuable, and he couldn't wait to do it again.

Greed

by L.B. Zinger

Max could barely contain his excitement. He had found treasure! There was a long silky fibre that felt very soft to him. He stuffed it into his pouch, sighing over the softness as he did so. This was a wonderful addition to his bed—the magnificent bed he had created with layer upon layer of such finds. His bed was a magical refuge in a mundane world.

His cubby was a wooden crate with mesh screening half way up the sides for ventilation and a flat wooden roof. He had an exit door that was kept closed and locked, but he had a back entrance where the wood had rotted and separated from the frame, just big enough for him to squeeze through. Each corner was specialised: one for food and water, one for elimination, one for his wonderful bed, and the last for his exercise wheel. The richness of his bedding and his treasury of gold, silver, and jewels made Max protect his space by hiding his stash in nooks and crannies—corners and crevices not visible to others.

He ran back to his cubby and squeezed himself through the back entrance. Hurriedly, he placed the fibre he had found in the bed, mixing it up with the other rags and sawdust to hide it from prying eyes. He saw no one else up and about—he couldn't believe his luck! The booty was his!

Next to the open trash bin, a woman's purse had tipped over with the contents spilling out. It was a mass of glorious things: shiny keys, a bracelet with tiny charms, some beaded earrings, a lipstick container, a small mirror, what seemed like a hundred nose tissues, and a wallet. There were some candies in an open container. Cautiously, he licked one. *Mint, yuck,* he thought and moved on.

Efficiency was key. Max went through the trove, delving deeper and deeper into the purse. Some beads were loose, and he captured those. The bracelet had a small cross and a little thimble on it, but he couldn't get them off. He left it. The mirror was wonderful, and he spent a few minutes gazing lovingly upon his reflection. It was too big for the pouch, but he decided that he must have it, even if he had to carry it back to his cubby the hard way. There was a book of matches, a battery, and a small bottle of something. The bottle cap was a little loose, and he shook out a drop. It did not taste like water and made his head funny. He left that too. Too much to carry.

Abandoning the purse, he turned to the trash. Every day there was something new and delicious. Today there was discarded meat, which smelled foul but wasn't on his shopping list anyway. Someone had thrown out half a bag of popcorn and some peanuts—a nice treat. There were also pieces of carrot and some peas. Must have been stew night at home. It all still smelled pretty good. Everything went into the pouch until it was stuffed and he could barely walk with all the food he was carrying. There was still more, and none of his neighbours had arrived.

His head swollen to three times its size, pouches overloaded, and breathless from exertion, he rolled the mirror back to his cubby and slid it through the slit in the wood. His cheeks were too full to get his head through, so he unloaded all of the hard items and one by one pushed the treasures through the opening. He was tired but knew he had to go back if he wanted more from this goldmine before the others found it. The secret compartment he had carved in the floor under his exercise wheel wasn't full. He started loading it with his newfound treasures, all the while watching for prying eyes.

Four or five trips later, he had almost filled his cache and fully exhausted himself. He put the food away and crawled into his wonderful bed, pulling the silk fibres over him as he dropped into a sound sleep, gazing at his mirror.

Sometime in the middle of his sleep, he heard soft steps and whispers outside his cubby. He growled, he hoped convincingly, and the steps faded away. It was his neighbours looking to steal from him. He would have to find a weapon. Maybe it would mean venturing out in the daytime when everyone else was asleep, to see if he could find a can top or a shard of glass to use as a weapon. No matter, he consoled himself, he could sort it out when he woke up.

At dusk, Max opened his eyes to the fading sunlight. With the breeze that wafted in, he could smell everyone's elimination dumps. He shivered. That smell was sure to attract the cleaners, who would come through and disturb everything. They had taken his things before, but this time, he would make sure that everything was well hidden.

Paranoid, he began packing up the shiny baubles that he had left out to admire and stashed them under his cubby. The mirror didn't fit anywhere, so he rolled it under the sawdust near his food. He took the silky string from last night and, with reluctance, stowed it in his safe place. There was some room for more, so he started thinking about who had things he might want.

He looked down the line of cubbies. Liz had a new

string of beads just hanging off her window frame. They seemed neglected, as if she didn't really want them. He squeezed as close as he could to the screen separating them and stretched out to touch them. Plastic! Plastic was tacky! Even if she had discarded them, those beads were not worth the effort of retrieving them.

Shaking his head at the tawdriness of his fellows, he turned to the other side where One-Eye lived. What was he doing? He saw One-Eye holding up a tiny silver thimble. Was that the charm from that bracelet? How did he get it off?

One-Eye held up a gold cross and a small diamond pendant. He turned to Max and nodded, as if saying to him: "See, I got your treasure. I was smart enough and strong enough to remove these when you weren't able to."

Max felt a surge of anger, then craftiness took over. One-Eye would go out sometime and he, Max, would sneak over and see what else One-Eye had stashed. For months, he had watched the old guy hiding stuff. When One-Eye left, he would clean him out. He wasn't particularly worried about detection—One-Eye's remaining eye was clouded with a large cataract. Max would roll in a few of One-Eye's blankets, leaving his scent just to taunt him, and have a good laugh at his expense.

Max sank down in his bed again, thinking of One-Eye's stash. He nodded off a bit, only vaguely aware of the noises of the community: children laughing, the squeak of a wheel going round, and the occasional grunts and growls of adults commingling.

When it was fully dark, Max got out of bed. He made a stop in his elimination area, then headed to the food and water section. The water tasted stale; he would have to do something about that. The best way to get fresh water was to empty the container out the window just before the cleaners got there. That way he would get clean water without fouling his cubby. Then he found some nice pieces of carrot and apple to have for a snack, topped off with the peanuts and popcorn he had found last night. The fuzzy stuff on the popcorn tasted metallic and stuck to his teeth. He spat out as much as he could, then gnawed on a few nuts to clean his teeth.

Out of the corner of his eye, Max saw One-Eye shuffle off towards the trash can. Quickly, he slid out his back door and over to One-Eye's cubby, approaching from the rear so that he wouldn't be seen. Peering in, he saw a mess: trinkets and baubles everywhere and loose strands of metallic threads and fibres crisscrossing the floor. The battery and matches he had seen last night were on the floor too. One-Eye had found Max's treasure pile and made off with more than Max had!

He knelt down to find a way in, but then Max's nerve froze. Suddenly, he was afraid to sneak into the cubby, but through the mesh, he was just able to reach some of the baubles and roll them to his hands. Stowing them quickly in his pouch, he looked up to see that One-Eye was making an unsteady shuffle back to his home. Max scurried through his back door and shoved the items into his cache. He sat back on his haunches and tried to look nonchalant. He would take inventory later.

"How are you today, One-Eye?" Max said, in a friendly tone.

Head up, One-Eye cast a rheumy glance towards the sound of the noise. *Boy, he is losing it,* Max thought. To think that this was the patriarch of the community. He took a hard look at what age had done to the old fellow: patchy hair, clouded eye, probably loss of hearing, since One-Eye hadn't responded to him. How the mighty had fallen.

"Were you in my shelter?" One-Eye's voice cracked and shuddered. Max shook his head, then realising One-Eye couldn't see that, cleared his throat to answer.

"Must have been kids. It wasn't me." He tried to keep the laughter and scorn out of his tone. Max crawled up on the frame of his wheel, which he had wedged in place with sticks for this purpose: to be able to see the cubbies around him better. One-Eye was emptying his pouches onto the floor and not only were there nearly whole baby carrots and pieces of apple, but more beads and jewellery. Max shook his head. How had Max missed what the blind senior citizen was able to find? It wasn't right.

Cynically, Max wondered what would happen when One-Eye died. It was clear that he was fading rapidly and probably would not last another winter. Was there a way that Max could rescue One-Eye's treasure before anyone else did? He had watched One-Eye hide it all while exercising on his wheel. No one would directly attack One Eye, out of respect, but if he died, well, then everything he had was up for grabs. As the resident of the closest cubby, Max could get there first. He would have to be alert for when the raspy breathing of his neighbour stopped. Another reason to stay on guard, even when sleeping.

Dawn came, and wearily, Max crawled back into bed. Aside from his trip to check out One Eye's stores, the night had been somewhat boring. He catalogued his treasures in his head as he drifted off to sleep. There was so much hidden away for his pleasure, and so much more he could liberate from One Eye. He felt good.

He didn't feel so good midway through his sleep,

when he was rudely awakened by the cleaners who rousted him from his bed and herded him into a common pen with the others. Each cubby was stripped down to the wooden floors and new sawdust put down. Beds were dismantled and hoarded food taken away. The cleaners expressed disgust over the collection of mouldy and desiccated foodstuffs and made a particular fuss over Max's home. They even found his cache under the flooring.

Max looked on aghast as his treasures were plundered and confiscated. Words like "junk" and "filth" trickled over to his ears. He stood against the wall in terror. His brain screamed. The best he could do was throw himself against the wall and pound it with his fists.

"No! No! No!" he croaked. The others looked at him derisively, and some even laughed. He almost cried at the lack of respect. He was the richest of all of them. It was envy that made them treat him this way.

The final blow came when the cleaners brought in fresh wood and nails and began repairing the cracks and crevices he had so carefully crafted to escape the cubby. Every cubby was repaired, so no one would be able to roam freely after the cleaners were done. They would be caged animals again. The smell of fresh wood made Max nauseous. Nothing would be the same.

Finally, they were taken back to their cubbies in a sad state. Max surveyed the devastation. There was clean water in his dispenser and clean food in his larder. There was clean sawdust on the floor. A few threads of his bedding remained, but the glorious silken fibres were gone. His elimination area was freshened, and the whole area smelled of citrusy disinfectant. It was sickening. He wanted to cry. They had even found his hiding place under the wooden floor. Empty!

Dismayed, he looked across at One-Eye's cubby. Surely Max was not alone in his torment. The old man had an even bigger stash than he did. His jaw dropped in shock. One-Eye was calmly rebuilding his bedding with stuff that had been hidden under the flooring and in the corners of the shelter. Some items had even been stashed in the walls of the shelter itself, now pulled into sight using a fine thread that Max was barely able to make out. He swore that One Eye bore a self-satisfied smirk.

The old one turned and gave him a rheumy stare, then winked with his good eye as he got on his squeaky wheel. Around his neck was the silk fibre Max had treasured and on it hung a tiny gold cross. As he passed by Max's window, wheeling faster and faster, he gave Max a wink and held one tiny finger up in the air.

Max took to his bed in frustration. For two days and

nights, he didn't get out of bed, listening to the squeak of One-Eye's wheel and the raspy breathing that went with it. On the third night, he heard a thump as the wheel stopped in mid-motion. He pulled himself up and looked out. One-Eye lay still on the floor. The raspy breathing was gone, and there was no movement. It was time for Max to restore his stash. But how to get out?

Max knew that the floor under the elimination area was weak. It was disgusting but he immediately began poking, digging, and chewing his way out. It took forever, but it was still night when he was able to make a hole and crawl out of his cubby. Sniffing, he followed One-Eye's scent, since it was disorienting to crawl under the cubbies.

Under One-Eye's cubby, the scent of something sweet and sticky was strong, mixed with that of the old guy. Boy, did he smell bad! Max looked around for a clue on how to get into the cache. He knew there was a hint under there somewhere. He remembered the fine thread that One-Eye had pulled to get at his things. Without thought, he brushed at a spiderweb in front of his face. Wait a minute! That was it! He gave a mighty tug on the string that was hanging down in front of him.

The Fire Department was summoned for what they

called, laughing, a minor explosion due to faecal material. The cleaners insisted that everything had been freshened that day but could not explain the battery wrapped in silver wires, the empty bottle of airline vodka, and the matches that had somehow survived the explosion and fire. The children were devastated at the death of two of their favourite hamsters.

The Package

by M. Sydnor Jr.

"We did it! I told you. I fucking told you!" Jimmy yelled from the passenger seat, drumming the dashboard with his hands.

"Yeah, that went better than expected." Simeon leaned over from the driver's seat and gave Jimmy a playful shove.

"Fuck yeah, it did. Five minutes. In and out. Boom. Now, we're set for life, brother. No more punching the fucking clock. No more following orders. I'm going to the Bahamas and never fucking coming back."

"In time, man. Don't want to raise suspicion." Simeon was the level-headed one. Calm, but super paranoid, constantly looking at his side and rear-view mirrors. They were in the middle of nowhere, but still… "Gotta lie low for a while."

"Lie low?"

"Low profile. Stay quiet. Stay clean. Follow the rules. That kind of lie low."

"Chill, man. Everything went as planned."

"Yeah, it—" Simeon looked up the road. "The fuck

is he doing?"

"What?"

"There!" Simeon pointed ahead.

On the other side of the road, coming towards them, a semitruck slowly veered into their lane.

"Probably just some old trucker," Jimmy suggested. "Pulling an all-nighter."

"Should we tag him?"

"No, man. We gotta ditch the gloves—the masks— and hide the package. We don't have time for this. We'll just call it in, all right? Let highway patrol deal with it."

"Fine. I just don't—"

"Sim! We just got the biggest score of our lives, and you're worried about some swerving truck in the middle of nowhere."

"He's in my lane, man. He's in my fucking lane." Simeon veered the car off the road onto the side dirt.

"Hey, hey! Move! Move!" Jimmy yelled as the truck kept on towards them.

"Whoa!"

"Watch out—"

The truck took claim to the opposite side of the road, with complete disregard for any other vehicles in the vicinity. It seemed to be drawn to the police cruiser as the grill of the semi smashed into the driver's side headlight and sent the car spinning out of control. Simeon bounced around in his seat, from his headrest into the steering wheel, doing an okay job at shielding his face but a horrible job at protecting his head. Jimmy flew through the windshield. Then, after the car spun three or four times, it flipped…and flipped…and flipped. Simeon's head smashed and cracked his side window, then he blacked out.

When Simeon opened his eyes in a hospital bed, he didn't see his wife, nor any family or friends. Just a woman standing on one side, who he assumed was a nurse, and a man on the other side, who he guessed was an officer. He knew the look; he was one of them.

"Welcome back to the land of the living, Officer Ray," the man said.

Simeon had a crazy headache and was sore all over. He tried to talk but couldn't. His throat felt full of something hard and uncomfortable; he choked, then tugged at whatever was in his mouth. Beeping sounds sped up, so did his breathing. The nurse pulled the tube out of his mouth. He gagged, then spat, then coughed.

The man didn't have a pleasant face, had a look that reminded him of his grade school teachers right before they'd send him to detention. So, with the headache came stress. He didn't worry about where his wife was or the status of his partner, only the contents of his trunk. Was he in trouble? Was this man here to arrest him?

"I'm Detective Brown. I'm here to grab a statement on what happened a few days ago. You understand?"

Sim nodded.

"Do you remember what happened? The accident?"

Sim was relieved, felt the weight of the world lift from his chest, and he took a deep breath. He took his time and recounted what happened. As planned, he and Jimmy had an excuse for being out in the country the way they were. They signed off on escorting an inmate to prison and they were on their way back from that when it happened. Driver likely fell asleep at the wheel and crashed into them. It was as simple as that.

The detective agreed. Even went as far as to suggest the driver was drunk and headed for them. No mention about the events after dropping the prisoner off, no mention about the state of the car or its contents.

Simeon figured they were in the clear but was reminded of a horrific scene in which his partner was thrown from the vehicle just before he blacked out. "Jimmy?" he asked.

Detective Brown sighed and dropped his head.

"Sorry. Your partner was pronounced dead at the scene. But the trucker has been arrested, and the department has taken legal action against the trucking company."

Simeon and Jimmy weren't the best of friends. Just partners stuck together with the same level of greed and corruption. Partners in crime.

The detective finished jotting down notes in his book and closed it. "That'll be all. Get better, son." He patted Simeon on his legs and left the room.

Mary ran in just as the nurse followed the detective out. "Oh, my God. You're up, you're okay. You're okay." She collapsed onto his stomach, kissed his cheeks, his lips, his chest, and squeezed him with no regard for his injuries.

"Ow, ow." It hurt more on the inside, but her embrace of love soon superseded that pain. "I'm good, babe. I'm good."

"I leave for two seconds, and you decide to wake up."

Simeon chuckled. It hurt to laugh, but it was good to see a friendly face. A lovely face. "How long have I been out?"

"Four days."

Four days? Shit! "So, what's happening? That detective didn't tell me much?" Mary always had an interest in his work. Always wanted to know details about everything: what he was up to, where he'd be patrolling. So, he knew she had a leg up on the crash and if there was an investigation into him and Jimmy.

She lifted herself off his waist and straightened her back, then she stretched her mouth into this great big smile. Something was up. "Well…your union got you a big-ass payday, that's what's happening. The trucking company they threatened to sue—they're settling."

"What?"

"One million dollars, baby." It was hard for her to contain her excitement.

"Umm, *what?*" He was speechless. His mind was a mess, but it was a jumble of positivity. The worry and stress of the accident left his mind, the death of his partner forgotten, the corruption that he'd participated in…no more. The headache…gone. He was smiling with her, mirroring her excitement, and they hugged.

A day later, he was released from the hospital and sent home. On top of the settlement from the trucking agency, the force gave him paid leave for six months. Other than a concussion, few broken ribs, a sprained wrist, some cuts, he was okay. But psychologically?

Before they even received the settlement money, Mary was travel planning, house shopping, building an Amazon wish list so long and extensive that she added things twice. Simeon loved to see her happy and busy, and he sat back while she made plans for their future. She wanted him to quit the force, retire, which made sense but he hadn't even considered it. The half-dozen times she'd asked him the following week leaving the hospital, he shrugged and said, "I'll think about it."

That thought always led to the accident, his partner Jimmy, their misdeeds, mainly their last one. And that thought sprouted into this big thing that troubled his mind, even clouded the million dollars that he'd receive, tax-free. That settlement would be enough to do absolutely nothing for the rest of his life. But that package, it tugged at him. Pulling his mind away, darkening his heart, mixing into a horrible idea that he couldn't help but entertain.

Simeon could justify this awful plan to retrieve the package to honour Jimmy's death, but he didn't care for him that much—partners in crime was the extent of their relationship. No honour amongst them.

After making some calls, he'd found out that the car was still at the impound. They would've found the package by now if they were on to him, to them. But here he was, enjoying his freedom, recovering from his injuries.

So, as his wife continued to plan their future, Simeon plotted, obsessing over this package tucked deep away in his trunk.

After Mary had fallen asleep, Simeon drove to the impound. It was a Sunday night, and he knew there'd be minimal security stationed there. His plan was to bullshit an excuse to the guard to look at the damages of his police cruiser. If that didn't work, plan B was to sneak in, find the car, pop the trunk, retrieve the package and the other evidence, then sneak out. When he arrived, he saw the guard stationed in the stall and smiled. He knew him.

Baron, a young guy with an extended family that knew Simeon's. He liked Baron, more than Jimmy, that's for sure. He approached the gate, the booth, knocked on the window, and smiled.

"Ay, Sim! What's up, man?"

"Insomnia, Baron. Insomnia."

The young guard chuckled. "I heard about what happened. Sorry! I didn't know Jimmy but heard he was a good man."

"Yeah. Thanks. I gotta be quick, don't want the wife waking up wondering where I went."

"I hear ya."

"Just wanted to take a look at my ride. I'm missing a few things and wanted to check if they're in the glove box or something."

"Oh yeah, man. Of course." Baron turned and grabbed a key from a wall, then gave it to Simeon. "Here ya go. It's in the back corner, lot seven."

He grabbed the keys and saluted him. "I'll be outta your hair in no time."

"Take your time, boss." Baron waved him off and returned to his chair with a book.

As Simeon made his way to the back, he didn't see any other guards around. The flashlight on his phone led him. *Quick and easy.*

In the last aisle, lot seven, he saw his cruiser at the end of the line. He took a deep breath and almost had a change of heart. *This is fucking stupid.* But the package, its contents corrupted his good conscience, and he imagined the possibilities once he had it in his possession. Fuck the legit one million dollars that would take care of him, his wife, and any babies they wanted to have. No one would question that, look into it. Investigate. He would be in the clear. He *was already* in the clear. But greed had a hell of a grip on his soul. It squeezed all common sense out of him, and before he realised, it had pushed him to the back of the damaged cruiser.

He unlocked the trunk, popped it, and saw that the authorities had already cleaned it out. He propped the phone on the ledge of the trunk so that he could see, then he reached in the back and pulled. The flooring came out and revealed a secret compartment behind the spare tire. He grabbed the first bag, unzipped it, and saw the gloves, face mask, and semiautomatic pistol with the serial number scratched off. The second bag, deeper in the hole, was smaller, lighter and inside were the diamonds he and Jimmy intercepted from a cartel carrier. Worth fifty million dollars.

The beauty of the diamonds mesmerised him. When they'd taken it from the cartel member, they hadn't had a chance to look at them, examine them, but as those diamonds spread across his palms, their glitter and shine made his eyes water. He knew this was the right decision. And he stood by it. And he had no regrets.

"Sir!" a voice called out.

It startled him, and he turned, still holding the diamonds, and saw another guard.

A flashlight moved from Simeon's face to his hands, and the officer gasped. "What in the world—"

Simeon didn't wait to see how he was going to react to a fellow police officer holding fifty million dollars' worth of diamonds in his hands at one o'clock in the morning. He grabbed the pistol and shot the guard twice in the chest. The shots were so loud, they bounced off the vehicles, some with alarms. The lights around the field lit up, voices erupted, more voices than Simeon accounted for on a Sunday night.

He zipped up the bag of diamonds, stuffed them in his pocket, and left the way he came in. The pistol in front of him, ready. Nothing in the world mattered more than escaping. The diamonds blocked away anything else. Being caught alive with these diamonds was not an option.

Simeon shot the next guard that confronted him, and the next one right after that. *Can't be more than three guards tonight. Can't be.* Then, he saw two coming from the front, so he fled behind a row of trucks before their flashlights could catch him. Once they passed, he crept behind them and put them both down.

He could see the front gate now, but he heard sirens in the distant. And he saw Baron holding his ground at the exit.

"Sim—Simeon!" He saw disbelief in the kid's eyes. Hurt. Shame. But most of all, confusion.

But Simeon was void of Simeon. Blame the diamonds because he didn't know this kid in front of him anymore. Without hesitation, he shot the kid in the head and carried on.

Once he made it past the gate, a dozen cop cars surrounded him. They saw him, he saw them. They pleaded for his surrender.

He wasn't going to be taken alive with those diamonds. So, he raised his gun.

Ashes to Ashes

by Eddie D. Moore

The estate sale auctioneer tapped the podium with his hammer and introduced the next lot. "Two of these urns are over one hundred years old. The other three are more recent, but if you research the names, you'll discover that you own a piece of this county's local history and folklore."

Jerry went to every court-ordered estate sale that one of his banks profited through. He had everything he wanted in life—piles of money, a large three-storey house, and influence. The auctions always provided the opportunity to buy something he'd really cherish owning, and that was something someone else wanted.

A thin grin slid onto Jerry's face when he heard muffled sobbing from the house's previous owner's wife. Her husband whispered something into her ear and lifted his bidding paddle. The auctioneer accepted the opening bid of fifty dollars and searched the attendants for a higher offer.

Jerry ground his teeth in frustration when he realised that no one else was going to bid. Judging by the whispers of the people close to him, it appeared that everyone had agreed to let the previous owners have the urns uncontested. He sighed and thought to himself sarcastically, *how freaking touching.*

The auctioneer blinked twice in surprise as Jerry raised his paddle and swallowed before acknowledging the new bid. His pause revealed that the auctioneer was aware of the crowd's plan on letting the family have the urns, so Jerry made a mental note to make sure that this man never worked for them again. Letting the urns pass through the auction uncontested was nothing short of stealing their fair value from the bank, and his anger flared as the previous owners made a pathetic attempt to outbid him.

Jerry doubled the man's bid and bit his lip to keep from laughing when the man threw his paddle on the ground and turned to comfort his grieving wife. The people sitting around Jerry sneered and gave him disapproving glances. Jerry shrugged and said just loud enough for them to hear, "You heard the man—local history and folklore. How can you put a value on that?"

Excitement boiled inside Jerry's chest as he loaded the urns into his trunk. Not only was he leaving with something that someone else desired, but he had upset the plans of dozens of people to get it. He couldn't wait to display them on the mantel above his fireplace, where he could gaze upon them every morning.

As Jerry got into his dark green Jaguar XE, the previous owner broke away from his wife's side and ran to Jerry's car. As Jerry drove away, he tapped on the window and shouted, "I need to warn you about the urns!" Jerry pushed the gas pedal a little harder and laughed when he saw the man wiping grass off his shirt in the rear-view mirror.

The artwork on the two oldest urns was stunning. They were carved from a solid piece of wood and inlaid with odd symbols made of brass, pewter, and bone. Jerry loved old furniture and knew that the inlay was a French technique called marquetry. A little research online revealed that the urns contained the ashes of Catherine de Chantraine and her stepbrother, Gilles.

Shunned by their family, Gilles and Chantraine had moved to the Colonies in 1727 and were soon married in a small ceremony under a full moon. When the remains of two missing youths were found on their property, Gilles and Chantraine were both charged with witchcraft and cannibalism. Two days later, they were burned at the stake by an angry mob while their children watched.

Jerry closed his laptop and shook his head. He walked to the mantel, picked up one of the old urns, and admired the inlay. He gave the top an experimental twist and shook his head when it didn't move. For a moment, he considered prying the top off with a knife, but he didn't want to damage it, so he tried again with a little more force.

The top popped off with a snap, dumping ashes over Jerry's hand and onto his pants. To his surprise, the ashes felt warm and fresh. He swept up the ashes and put them back into the urn. He gently placed the urn back on the mantel and said softly, "They must've got hot in my trunk." He kicked back in his recliner, relaxed, and closed his eyes.

Jerry's eyes popped open when he smelt smoke. Heart racing, Jerry looked around the room, but there was no fire. The flames were only visible in the mirror. He stood up as he saw someone on fire running through the flames. Chills ran up his spine when he heard screams and cackling laughter. He took a step towards the mirror, but a wave of heat drove him back.

He spun when he heard someone chanting in French behind him, but no one was there. When he looked into the mirror, he saw a woman with horrible burns standing beside him. He turned to run but fell to the floor as the chair beside him exploded in flames. He felt unseen hands took a hold of him, and a moment later, burns appeared on his arms where they gripped him.

Jerry screamed, "Let me go! I'll give you anything! What do you want?"

The flames spread and filled the room as a feminine voice with a French accent softly answered, "Only what was lost, life."

Serving Others

by Dawn Knox

Father Stithbeorht placed his hand over Gytha's mouth to keep her quiet. For such a bulky man, he was surprisingly swift and had reacted at the first knock on his bedroom door.

"Wait!" he shouted sharply. "I am at my devotions."

"There are two men here to see you, Father," a muffled voice called from the hall.

"Give them beds for the night. I will see them on the morrow."

"They say they will speak with you tonight, Father. They are most insistent."

"Very well! They must wait until my prayers are finished." With a batting movement of his ringed fingers, he signalled to the girl to get out of bed and go, indicating she should leave by the passage at the back of his bedroom. She pulled her clothes on quickly then turning, she grabbed a chunk of cheese, the loaf, and an apple and walked swiftly to the passage. As she disappeared through the doorway, she glanced briefly over her shoulder at the Abbot and laughed.

There was no time to teach her a lesson. She was young and light on her feet and would be at the end of the passage, then out in the countryside before he could catch her. Besides, he had to dress and remove his rings and the ruby cross from around his neck before he received the Bishop's men. He put the jewellery under his pillow, slipped on his habit, and picked up his rosary. The next time he demanded the villagers send him a girl, he would insist on Gytha and he'd punish her then.

"This had better be important to have disturbed my prayers," he said in a menacing voice to Brother Oswulf as he opened the door.

"They swear they'll see you tonight, Father, on the orders of the Bishop. I tried to delay them, but they'd have none of it. I've given them refreshments and they're waiting in the refectory."

Father Stithbeorht, clutching his rosary, pushed past the young monk.

"God be with you this night, gentlemen. What business brings you to St Alfgar?"

Beads of sweat stood out on his forehead. The Bishop never sent messengers with good news.

"God be with you, Father Abbot," said the taller of

the two men. "My apologies for disturbing you at such a late hour but St Alfgar is further from civilisation than my companion and I understood. We underestimated the time it would take to reach you. However, the Bishop was most keen for us to collect the taxes you owe."

"But we've only just paid the year's taxes! Surely the Bishop understands we are a poor community which espouses poverty, chastity, and obedience… We share our meagre food with the villagers. There is very little to spare."

The messenger tugged his beard thoughtfully. "As you say, the monks appear to be half-starved. Yet you, Father Stithbeorht, seem very well fed…" His gaze moved slowly down the portly figure of the Abbot and rested on his paunch.

Father Stithbeorht sucked in his stomach and tucked his plump fingers into the sleeves of his habit. "God bestows his goodness on those who are most abstemious. Brother Oswulf will testify to the fact that my rations are half of my brothers'. Nevertheless, God sees fit to feed my body and soul."

"Indeed!" the messenger said. "Then if God provides for the abstemious, He will surely give you the wherewithal to provide the taxes you owe our Lord Bishop." The messenger picked up the tankard and drank deeply, all the while keeping his eyes fixed on the Abbot's face.

In the morning, Father Stithbeorht gave the Bishop's men a golden crucifix as payment for the abbey's debts.

"As you said, Father, God provides for those who are the most self-denying," the messenger said, tucking the golden cross into his saddlebag. "My Lord Bishop will be most pleased at your abstemiousness!"

The Abbot could not bring himself to reply.

"Farewell," the messenger said with a cheerful wave. "We will return in six months."

"Six months?" Abbot Stithbeorht said. "But—"

His words went unheard as the two riders urged their horses forward and galloped away.

So, the Bishop intended to squeeze as much out of St Alfgar as he could. It was time for him to move on. Abbot Stithbeorht had safely hidden all the treasures his predecessor had left, in a strong chest with a lock which required two keys to open it—two keys which he possessed. The wealthy abbey had yielded many valuables that the newly installed Father Stithbeorht removed in a show of piety, declaring them an obstacle to true worship. From time to time, when the crops failed, he'd been forced to sacrifice a small item to prevent the entire community from starvation. But now the Bishop was becoming greedy, the Abbot would have to take steps to safeguard the hoard. If he travelled far enough, he would set up again, out of the clutches of any Bishops. There were always idealistic, young men who yearned for a life of service and piety—men with strong backs and large, capable hands who were trusting and obedient. The Abbot would find them and set up a new abbey.

St Alfgar and the outlying village were cut off for many months during the long and bitter winter, while the ground resisted all efforts of spade or pickaxe and no early crops were sown. Rats sought the relative warmth of stables, hovels, and monks' cells, bringing disease and death to those who hadn't already starved. The Abbot, dreading the Bishop's men would return before spring, set off one frosty morning ostensibly to petition the Bishop, and Brother Oswulf offered to accompany him, saying the journey during this time of deprivation would be hazardous and he would give up his life to protect Father Stithbeorht. The Abbot had thanked him and assured him his offer would not go unnoticed by the Almighty.

"However," the Abbot had said, "I have faith that God will protect me and deliver me unharmed to the Bishop who will surely assist us in our hour of need."

The Abbot set off with several large bags of supplies inside which he hid his treasures.

"I may need to offer this food to the poor and hungry on my journey," he said, and although the emaciated monks watched him through sunken eyes, they nodded in approval at his generosity.

"Brother Oswulf is in charge until such time as God sees fit to allow me to return, Brothers. And remember, our order is founded on poverty, chastity, and obedience at all times."

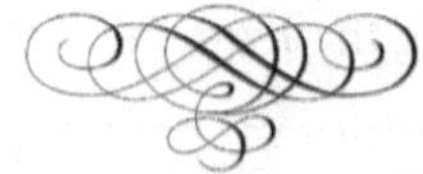

By late summer, the Abbot had not returned, and over half the monks had died of starvation or sickness. The village folk had suffered too, and many had succumbed to fever. Brother Oswulf had not collected rents and had continued to leave food out for the villagers each evening, and in return, they'd shared their meagre crops and meat they'd trapped or hunted with the monks.

In honour of Father Stithbeorht, the Brothers piled small rocks one on top of the other—in much the same way as a drystone wall is built—outside the abbey's walls, so that they and the villagers could pay tribute to him. Not that the villagers took much notice. Each evening, Brother Oswulf carried food for the poor through the passage at the back of the Abbot's bedroom and placed it in the box which offered protection from marauding animals and allowed villagers to help themselves. By morning, the food was always gone and footprints in the mud or the snow showed a steady stream of people from the village, but the tracks never detoured to approach the small tribute.

The monks, however, tended the stone structure, replacing rocks which were dislodged by animals, birds, or the vicious wind, hoping it would guide the Abbot back to them. They'd wanted to send one of their number to the Bishop to look for the Abbot and accompany him home but the remaining horse was not strong enough to withstand the journey, and although several monks volunteered to go by foot, they were also too weak.

One day, a young woman approached Brother Oswulf as he repaired the stones. He recognised her as Gytha, the blacksmith's daughter.

"Still trying to grow rocks?" she asked, her lip curled in contempt. "Your time'd be better spent tending your fields than honouring that man." She spat, and a gob of spittle splattered against one of the lower stones.

"Ungrateful wretch!" Brother Oswulf said. "You were always there, ready to take the food he left for the villagers each evening! And after his generosity, you refuse to show him respect! Clear off!"

"Generosity? Did you see what he put out for us so *generously* each evening?"

"Yes, Mistress Gytha, I did. I delivered it to his room each day," Brother Oswulf said, his lips clamped tightly together in disapproval. He'd vowed to dedicate his life to poverty, chastity, and obedience, but there were no rules against knocking some respect into the girl, and he bunched his fists.

"You may have delivered food to *him*, but did you see how much of it he actually put out for *us*?"

Brother Oswulf narrowed his eyes. "Slanderous woman!"

"Not so," she said, with a smile, although her eyes glinted hard and bright. "He ate his fill before leaving us the bones and crumbs."

"I shall teach you a lesson! Father Stithbeorht is the finest of men!" Brother Oswulf raised his hand to strike the woman, but she stepped nimbly out of his reach.

"The finest of men!" she mimicked his voice, her hands on her hips and a mocking smile on her face. "Tell me, is it you who now sleeps in his bed with the fine woollen blankets and the beautiful green hangings? Do you hold the two keys for the ornate chest with the huge lock which lies next to the bed?"

Brother Oswulf's hand froze in mid-air, his eyes moving across Gytha's insolent face. How did she know? Had someone described the room to her? A lucky guess? Few entered the Abbot's room which Brother Oswulf found disturbingly ostentatious. The Abbot insisted God had directed him to keep his predecessor's belongings, despite them disturbing him too. He said he'd pleaded with their Heavenly Father to be rid of them but to no avail… And God's will must be done.

Brother Oswulf lowered his hand slowly. "How do you know this, wench?"

She threw back her head and laughed. "How d'you think? And I'm not the only woman who knows—Have you not noticed children in the village with the same colouring as Father Stithbeorht!"

Brother Oswulf's voice was no more than a whisper, and he shook his head. "No, you lie! Somebody told you what was in the Abbot's room. I cannot believe after all his tireless work for the village, you speak so ill of him!"

"Believe what you like!" she said with a toss of her head. "But I think you'll find the villagers have helped the abbey more than the abbey has ever helped the village. You may grow cabbages and onions but when we trap a few rabbits, we share them with you. You'd all have starved if it wasn't for us—with or without your precious

Abbot."

She suddenly caught her breath as if having noticed a joke and threw her head back and laughed heartily, then turning on her heel, she strode away towards the woods and the village. Brother Oswulf watched her go, striding energetically, a picture of health. How could that be? Food had been so scarce. He and his brothers were skinny and lethargic, many with sores and scabs. The Abbot had been quick to turn villagers off the abbey's land if they failed to pay their rents on time which had not seemed charitable to Brother Oswulf but he'd never questioned it. *Obedience to the Abbot at all times.* Father Stithbeorht usually raised the rents after harvest, and Brother Oswulf was dreading the time. The crops were poor this year, and he couldn't imagine turning people out of their homes, but if the Abbot returned and found he'd failed in his duties...

Brother Oswulf decided to walk into the village and see how bad the conditions were. But surprisingly, although the population had dwindled after fever spread through the area, the remaining population was healthy, and there was an air of plenty about the place. The sails on the windmill had been mended, and there were sacks of flour visible through the door as the monk passed.

The last time he'd visited the village, the children had gripped their mothers' skirts and observed him with enormous eyes set in pinched faces, their stick-thin limbs clad in rags. But now, dirty children rolled and played down by the river, splashing in the shallows, full of energy. Even the dogs appeared well-fed. Brother Oswulf crossed himself. Was there witchcraft at work here? They lived not a mile from the abbey, so how could they have enough while the monks starved?

As Brother Oswulf turned to go back to the abbey, he saw a man he recognised, coming towards him on the path. Eric was slower than the other villagers, prone to laughter at inappropriate moments, like a child in a man's body. He chatted to his goats as he guided them back to the pen for the night.

"Brother!" Eric said in salute, then giggled.

"Eric! Well met, indeed!" Brother Oswulf said, and taking the other man's arm, he added, "Stay awhile, I'd like to know how you and your family are faring during these difficult times."

"Well enough, thank you, Brother," Eric said, a puzzled frown on his face. "Times are good. Better'n they been for a while."

"Ah! And why is that?"

Eric looked about as if searching for an answer.

"The crops have been poor, and yet you all have enough to eat…" Brother Oswulf prompted.

"We's buying food from yonder town," Eric said, waving his hand towards the north.

"Buying?"

"Yes, Brother. It were because of the Abbot—"

"Abbot Stithbeorht gave you money?"

Eric's eyes widened, and he glanced about as if looking for an escape as he twisted his hat in his hands.

He was an honest man. Brother Oswulf knew Eric would tell the truth regardless of the consequences. And he suspected Eric knew something.

"Do you know where the Abbot went?" Brother Oswulf asked.

Eric drew in a sharp breath and glanced at the forge. His mouth grew slack, and a string of saliva dangled from his lip.

"Come, Eric," Brother Oswulf said in gentle tones, "tell me what you know…"

Eric gulped. "I been warned not to say…"

"But you can tell me, Eric…"

"W…well, it were Sibert." He nodded at the forge which lay empty since the death of the blacksmith during the outbreak of fever. "The Abbot's horse lost a shoe, and he came back here, but Sibert…" Eric looked about wildly as if hoping someone would rescue him.

"Yes?" said Brother Oswulf gently.

"He stole the Abbot's bags. Full of gold, they were! The Abbot cursed Sibert and said the Abbot who came to replace him in the abbey would raise the rents even higher."

"I see," said Brother Oswulf, "and after that, the Abbot left?"

Eric nodded. "Sibert chased him out. And then the fever came. And Sibert died."

"And what happened to the gold?" Brother Oswulf asked.

"Shared."

"The villagers shared it out?"

"Yes. All gone now. All gone…" Eric said, stepping backwards away from the monk, then abruptly, he ran towards the woods, followed by his goats.

Brother Oswulf turned to leave the village, his mind a riot of thoughts. Eric was incapable of lying, and yet it was hard to believe the Abbot had so much of value in his possession. Perhaps the girl had been right after all. Fragments of memories shifted, sliding against each other, until a picture formed. He'd believed the Abbot before, but now doubts filled his mind… One thing was certain, if Father Stithbeorht had no intention of returning, then Brother Oswulf was in charge and decisions needed to be made and changes implemented.

Gytha watched the exchange from the village barn. It had been lucky Eric hadn't been there when the Abbot rode through the village. Anticipating someone would ask Eric about the events that day, he'd been given a simplified version of what had really happened, so if asked, he could tell what he knew.

He hadn't been told the men had lain waiting to ambush the Abbot. There were brigands aplenty abroad at this terrible time, and who should say where an attack on a lone man might take place? The food, money, and valuables had been shared between the men as well as the guilt, each dealing with the Abbot as he saw fit to compensate for the extortionate rents and depravity with their women. Once divided, the food was not sufficient to feed hungry mouths for long, and someone had suggested it would be a shame to waste such prime meat as the Abbot. At first it had merely been a joke, but once it had taken root, the idea grew. Why not? The Abbot was little better than an animal, someone had said. And someone had added he might taste as good. Or perhaps better, someone else suggested. The body must be hidden and it would be a crime to simply bury such fresh meat…

People were too hungry to be exacting, and pots had

bubbled with meaty stew for the first time in months. But the villagers were not greedy, they'd shared their bounty with the Brothers in the abbey.

With a sardonic smile, Gytha thought the Abbot may have saved many lives, and for the first time, he'd served his Brothers by being served *to* his Brothers.

Charity Begins at Home

by Dawn DeBraal

Sister Mary Ellen Dustin was excited by the challenge Father Beck offered the Sisters of Perpetual Adoration. The Sisters had their favourite charities. Father Beck announced that the Sister, who raised the most funds in the next few weeks, would get her charity project fully funded.

Sister Mary Ellen wanted to host orphans from a different country, but the cost was high. She excitedly jumped into the contest. In her heart of hearts, she wanted to help orphans, but there was a part of her that couldn't turn down a good competition. She was born this way. Sister Elaine was still harping on her after-school gym program. Some silly sports program that allowed children whose parents worked until 6 p.m. to play at the gym in the Catholic school. Why would there be a cost for that program? Sister Elaine could just donate her time. The Sisters of Perpetual Adoration already had a gym and basketballs, so where was the cost? Sister Theresa Ann wanted to feed the poor, which had been done for hundreds of years. Feeding the poor was nothing new. No matter how long they fed the poor, they were back the next day asking for more! Sister Margaret Ann wanted to start a day care for teen mothers. Like the Catholic Church wanted to promote teen pregnancy. Sister Margaret Ann also had a hyper-need to compete. She saw the look and recognised it in Sister Mary Ellen. They both had the wickedness of greed, the desire to win in their souls. No amount of religious training or fervency would ever break the Sisters of this internal flaw.

Don't worry. We'll care for your bastard while you get an education. Sister Mary Ellen thought that should be Sister Margaret Ann's motto. Sister Mary Ellen knew that her cause was the best of all. She just needed to raise more money than the rest and spent the day running off pictures of children from Romania, with runny noses and crying faces. These children were not up for adoption, but she didn't care. Their lovely little faces showed just the right amount of pain and anguish. Those sad little faces would melt the hearts of even the meanest person, like Nanette Andersen. Nanette didn't have a soft bone in her body, especially when it came time to separate Nanette from her money, though Mrs Andersen was known to be well-off. Nanette didn't want for anything except a soul.

Sister Mary Ellen decided to go for the big fish in the pond. All the other Sisters could sell crocheted doilies or macramé plant hangers. Sister Mary Ellen was going to go for the jugular vein of the Sisters of Perpetual Adoration Catholic Church—Nanette Andersen. She felt confident in her plan.

Bright and early in the morning, the other Sisters shared their ideas of what they could do for fundraising. Sister Mary Ellen thought this was ridiculous. Why would you help one another and then split the donations? How would anyone win? The other Sisters invited Sister Mary Ellen, who quickly declined, saying she had ideas and wasn't going to get into a group with them.

The other Sisters seemed interested but perturbed. Without a clear winner, Father Beck would never extend the money to all of them. They hoped he would do so in the event of a tie. The Sisters could be very naïve. As per her plan, Sister Mary Ellen drove to Nadine Andersen's house. Nadine and her husband Greyson were filthy rich. You could see it in their home, in their clothing, the cars they drove. And they had been pretty generous to the Sisters of Perpetual Adoration. The Andersens funded the Sunday School program and the food drive. They also kept the academic school afloat. You'd think that was enough, but Sister Mary Ellen wanted to win her chance at the wheel of orphans.

She knocked on the Andersen door. No one answered. Hearing the noise of splashing and horseplay behind the house, Sister Mary Ellen walked around. She opened the backyard gate slowly when she saw Nadine in the pool with someone other than her husband. The Sister sensed victory in her future. She had what she needed on Nadine to garner her full support for her orphan project. Taking her cell phone out, Sister Mary Ellen heard the sound of the camera snapping several pictures before she closed the gate behind her.

If Nadine didn't fall in love with the fake children she brought with her to bring her to tears, she would no doubt do anything to prevent the compromising pictures of her dalliance in the pool from going out into the community. Sister left quietly. She would come back tomorrow.

When she got back to the convent, all the Sisters were curious as to how her plans went. Sister Mary Ellen just smiled saying, "Things couldn't have gone better!" She had a twinkle in her eye. That night after she said her prayers, she pulled out the phone, looking over what she had taken. She extended her hand through the back gate and shot a hundred pictures. She was so glad Sister Margaret Ann showed her how to do this when she asked the Sister how she took such lovely pictures.

Sister Mary Ellen sucked in a sharp breath when she found out the man in the pool was none other than Father Beck. How could she not see that at the time? Another intrusive thought entered her mind. The camera that told the truth, she could up her ante. She was going to ask for a few thousand. The picture was worth ten thousand words. Nadine was all over Father Beck in the pool. It was unmistakable. She had some wonderful pictures. Chuckling to herself, she silently thanked Sister Margaret Ann for helping her raise funds for the orphan children.

Nadine Andersen answered the door. She was pleasant enough. She invited Sister Mary Ellen in, providing her with a cool drink. Sister took out the fake orphan pictures—beautiful children with snotty noses and teary eyes. She had stories for each one. She let Nadine know she wanted to bring the orphans to the United States so that they could be adopted. But the cost was high.

Nadine sat stoically, eyeing the sad pictures that didn't move her. Not one bit. She told Sister Mary Ellen she was already giving for much of the church functioning and wasn't sure about the orphans. Sister Mary Ellen kept showing the pictures until the orphans ran out, and Nadine was looking at a picture of herself cavorting in the pool with Father Beck. Nadine was no longer so stoic.

"How did you get these?" she hissed. Sister Mary Ellen pretended not to understand why Nadine was so upset.

"Don't you think you could find your way to giving to the Romanian Orphan Fly?" Nadine glared at Sister Mary Ellen.

"How much would it cost to help the children?" she said stiffly.

"For all the ones I would like to bring over, about ten thousand dollars," Sister Mary Ellen said with a winning smile. Nadine swept up all the pictures and ran them through the paper shredder at her desk. She then pulled out her cheque book, writing one out for ten thousand dollars. She tore the cheque out, handing it to the Sister.

"I need your assurances that I will not see those pictures after today." Sister Mary Ellen assured Nadine that she would not see the pictures again.

Several weeks went by. The deadline loomed for the Sisters of Perpetual Adoration to get their final count of what they had collected for their favourite charity.

Father Beck came out to tell the Sisters there was a tie. Sister Margaret Ann and Sister Mary Ellen. He needed to think of how to break the deadlock. Father Beck told each Sister to prepare a presentation, and he would make the final decision. Sister Mary Ellen simply ran off the non-orphan Romanian crying children and threw a few pictures of Father Beck in the pool with Nadine Andersen. Sister Margaret Ann couldn't have collected ten thousand for a teen school day care centre. How had she pulled off raising ten thousand? Sister Mary Ellen thought that perhaps she shouldn't have been so confident. She probably should have seen fit to make some macramé pot hangers or crocheted doilies and try to increase her fundraising abilities. The Sister was so confident no one would raise as much money as she. Well, the good Father would see it her way, he'd have to go for her project because she had the "goods" on Father Beck.

Sister Margaret Ann came out of her presentation. She was quite confident she had won the Father over with her presentation.

Sister Mary Ellen sat down with Father Beck, as he turned over the presentation Sister Margaret Ann had just shown. He looked red-faced and upset.

"Please, show me what you have." Sister Mary Ellen started with the crying non-orphan Romanian children but then got to the pool pictures. Father Beck lost all colour in his cheeks. How could this happen? He thanked Sister Mary Ellen and told her he needed to think about this very seriously and would get back to her.

Sister Mary Ellen couldn't believe he would pretend

not to see the eight-inch by ten-inch colour photos of him in the pool with Nadine Andersen. Sister Mary Ellen left in a huff.

As Sister Mary Ellen and Sister Margaret Ann waited in the hall, they heard a single shot.

"Was that a gun?" The Sisters ran into the priest's office. Father Beck's forehead sported a single bullet hole. He had fallen forward on the desk, bleeding over the presentations. Both the Sisters were stunned. Sister Margaret Ann picked up the pictures of Nadine and Father Beck frolicking in the pool.

"Wow, I thought he was going to vote for me," snorted Sister Margaret Ann.

"How could you think that? I blackmailed Nadine Andersen over her infidelity with a priest for my orphaned children," Sister Mary Ellen snapped.

"I thought he was going to vote for my teen pregnancy school-sponsored day care centre. I blackmailed Father Beck for ten thousand dollars. He has impregnated Sue Ann Knavely. She is a sophomore in high school and will need day care for Father Beck's child, that's due any day now."

Both Sisters looked at one another with knowing eyes. One recognised herself in the other. Without saying a word to each other, they quickly gathered up their presentations, shredding only the offending evidence. Several other Sisters came running to the screams of the Sisters who found Father Beck had committed suicide. What a tragedy they had walked in on.

Mother Superior of the Sisters of Perpetual Adoration decided both charities, Sister Mary Ellen's "Orphan Fly" and Sister Margaret Ann's "Teen Day Care Centre" programs, would be funded equally. Mother Superior decided that the Sisters had tied fair and square and that Father Beck had not made his final decision before he put a bullet in his brain.

The Judas Kiss

by Zoey Xolton

Do it, whispered Lucifer.

Judas fingered the purse of thirty silver pieces hidden in his robe.

It is your destiny to rule in Hell, Judas. There are more pleasures to be had in the Infernal Kingdom than in all of Heaven and Earth. Join me.

Glancing at the Fallen Angel and then the armed apostates, he approached Jesus.

Jesus met his eye. "Do as you must."

Judas swallowed hard. His Lord had the gift of prophecy. Feeling the weight of the blood money, he kissed him—a betrayer's kiss.

At the signal, the apostates descended and Jesus arrested.

Lucifer smiled.

A Creature Born from Greed

by Majanka Verstraete

I want it all. I need it all. I deserve it all.

Father used to shower me with gifts—little knickknacks that were supposed to make up for how long he stayed away from home. The more demanding his job became, the fewer hours he spent at home, and the more lavish those gifts grew. By the time I was six years old, it was a handmade dollhouse he had spent half a fortune on. When I turned ten, he gave me my own pony. At twelve, he bought me a diamond necklace more expensive than any jewellery he had ever given my mother.

Father wanted to buy my affection, I realise now. He felt guilty for not being around more, for not being a good father; so whatever hole his lack of love left in my heart, he tried to fill it with gifts. Beautiful, extravagant *things*.

Things that unlike him couldn't one day wither and die.

Five years ago, burglars entered his penthouse near his office and stabbed him to death, leaving him to drown in a pool of his own blood.

Father left most of his estate to me, including our sprawling summerhouse and a hefty sum of money. If spent wisely, that money could probably last me a lifetime. Unfortunately, I had blown through it in just a few months' time. Mother was furious that she only inherited our house in the city and a much smaller part of his fortune.

The last time I spoke to my mother was a few months after the funeral, when she said those nasty things over the phone that kept echoing through my mind. *You're greedy. Selfish. Egotistical. You never loved me.*

As I'm soaking here in the bathtub on the second floor of the summerhouse, surrounded by a silence lingering between eerie and comforting, I think about my father, who was so desperate to fill that hole in my heart that he only ended up making the hole that much larger. He never understood that greed is a bottomless pit.

I raise my cigarette to my mouth, inhaling the fumes to try and calm down, and my thoughts drift to my mother. I haven't spoken to her since she shouted those hurtful words to me, but today, I feel like calling her.

As I breathe in the smoke, I think about my wedding day. I never really wanted to get married, but after Father passed away, when winter rolled into summer and the years inched by, my fortune shrinking with every passing month, I realised I had no choice. There was always something I wanted, something I *needed*. Another thousand-dollar purse, designer shoes, a house near the beach, despite detesting sand and the sea.

Simply put, I needed someone to pay for my extravagant lifestyle. For the things I deserved and *craved* like a starving man craves food. So, when I met Freddie, it was his wealth that drew me to him. The good looks were just a bonus. Our wedding was a beautiful affair costing roughly a hundred thousand dollars, and Freddie succumbed to all my whims. He was the ideal husband.

Emphasis on *was*.

I stub out my cigarette and drop it in the ashtray next to the bath. The water in the tub ran cold half an hour ago, but I can't bring myself to get up. Getting up means facing what I did, and I don't feel strong enough yet. Maybe I never will be. Maybe I should just soak in this bathtub forever.

Over the years, I began to realise Freddie's fortune wasn't as vast as he made me believe. He led a luxurious lifestyle, but he was burning through his money faster than a high-speed train racing between capitals. He tried to hide it from me at first, still giving into my every desire, but I began to notice the small cracks in his persona: the wavering smile that didn't reach his eyes, the panicked looked flashing across his face whenever I mentioned going on a shopping trip or buying a new car.

The last few weeks were horrible. He accused me of draining him, not just of money but also of love, like a vampire sucking its victim dry. I was draining the life out of him, he said during one of our many arguments.

All you do is want, he shouted at me. *I want this, I want this, and this! All you do is take and take, and you never give. Well, guess what, I don't have anything left to give either.*

I take a deep breath and sink deeper into the bathtub, letting my head rest beneath the surface. It would be so easy to just keep holding my breath until I die. Easier than getting up and having to face the mess downstairs.

But drowning yourself isn't easy. In fact, I wager it's near impossible. After holding my breath for as long as I can, instinct kicks in and forces me back above water.

I breathe in deep, nearly choking on the air entering my lungs. Yet, my almost-suicide-attempt makes me feel energised, awake. Despite the weight on my shoulders— *is it guilt?*—still pulling me down, I realise I have no choice.

I scramble out of the bathtub and take a towel to dry myself. Parts of the conversation between Freddie and I from earlier flash through my mind.

"It's almost our wedding anniversary," I reminded Freddie, several hours ago, when he walked in the house. He had just arrived home from work and had probably entered the parlour to pour himself a drink, one of his many habits I had got to know so well over the years. It was the first sentence I spoke to him. In fact, I had made sure I was in the parlour simply so I could discuss this matter with him; the glass of wine in front of me was just for show, giving me a reason to be here. I didn't want to wait until dinner so he could brush me off again, like he had done three days ago, when I first brought up the issue.

"I really think we should host a party," I said, sipping from the wine—a red vintage one from my father's collection. "The summerhouse is perfect for parties, but it needs some work to get into shape, don't you think?" Ask a question, make him think it was his idea instead of mine. "I want to give the place a makeover, bring it back to its former glory. I already spoke to an interior architect, and she—"

"What?" Freddie had ignored most of what I had said

so far, but he grimaced at me mentioning I had already discussed the matters with an interior architect. "Why would you do that?"

"We'll need an architect for a project like this, Freddie." I frowned at him. "We can't very well do it ourselves, can we? Anyway, the architect said that, with about two hundred thousand dollars thrown at it, we'll be able to kick the summerhouse back into shape."

Freddie nearly choked on the brandy he had poured himself. "Two…two hundred thousand?" His shock turned into a scowl in seconds. "No. I already told you this project was out of the question. We can't afford to spend two hundred thousand on a summerhouse. I know you inherited it from your father and that it's special, but—"

"Freddie," I interrupted him mid-sentence, giving him a dangerous glare. "You don't understand. I really *want* this. Consider it an anniversary gift. You don't have to buy me anything else, although, of course I wouldn't say no to that gorgeous diamond ring we saw at the jeweller's last month. Remember, when we got your watch fixed?" I tried to sound innocuous, tried to hide from him how much I craved this, needed this. Like a heroin addict hiding their drugs, I was an addict to spending, and I was desperate to hide how important it was to me.

"I don't know how I can make you understand this." Freddie shook his head, looking as panicked as a deer caught in the headlights of a car. "I'm not throwing an over-the-top party for our anniversary, and I'm not buying you a diamond ring." He scratched his neck. "Money is tight. I told you. I…I was thinking of buying you some flowers, and…"

"Freddie." My hand tightened around the wine glass. "We've been married for two years, and you want to give me *flowers*?"

"I know it's not very original." Freddie sighed and slumped down on the chair next to mine. He looked ten years older, every wrinkle more pronounced, his eyes sunken in their sockets.

Had my greed drained him so?

He reminded me of a mummy, a walking corpse.

"Or maybe we could do something together." He held open his hand, but I didn't take it, instead clinging on to the wine glass as if it was a lifeline in the open ocean. "Take a cooking class or something. It could bring us closer together."

Strangely enough, his eyes sparkled with hope. Hope for what? That I would say "yes"?

I cackled, the laugh escaping from my throat before

I could stop it. "A cooking class? Flowers? You think that's all I deserve, Freddie?" I summoned all my hatred, tried to stare him down as if he was nothing but an insect I could crunch under my heel. "I deserve more than that. So much more."

"Honey."

That stupid idiot was still trying.

"It's not that you don't deserve more, love," he said. "It's just that right now, I can't give you more." He sighed. "I can't give you what you want, love. Not this time."

What I want?

"It's not what I want, Freddie, it's what I *need*." I hadn't meant to say those words out loud, but I did.

My chest tightened, and my blood rushed to my ears. I hated him, the little worm. I despised the way he squirmed in his seat, terrified by my scrutinising glares. I could barely believe I had married this *insect* two years ago.

I shake my head to try and bury the memory of what happened earlier this evening. Back in the bathroom, I've put my nightgown on, operating on autopilot, and I realise that I have no choice but to go downstairs now.

Much needs to happen. Luckily, we don't have any servants staying overnight at the summerhouse, but by the time the cleaning lady comes on Wednesday, I need to get rid of all the evidence.

Dreading every step, I drag myself downstairs. Part of me hoped that the trail of blood at the entrance to the parlour would have magically vanished—that what transpired earlier did not happen at all, the dark thoughts just a figment of my imagination. But the blood staining the floor shows it really happened.

I killed Freddie.

The memory flashes in front of my eyes. I see my hand curling around the bottle of wine, half empty.

Standing up on wobbly legs, it all happened so fast. I smashed down the bottle on the table, and the bottle broke in half. Then, I plunged the bottle, sharp edges first, into Freddie's neck.

He screamed only once, then he reached for his throat, as if touching the wound would magically stop the bleeding. He slumped forward, the bottle still sticking in his neck.

I leaned back in my seat and took a sip of wine, watching as he bled dry.

The rage I felt back then returns to me now, as I see Freddie's corpse lying face down on the table in the parlour. I hate him so much. He's the one who caused all this, not me. He denied me—not once, but twice—and he suggested I tone down my desires, my greed.

I won't and I can't. Not for him. Not for anyone.

Luckily, most of the blood is located on the table; the trail from the parlour to the hallway was made by me when I went upstairs to take a bath. It will not be such a hassle to clean up this mess as I feared.

Freddie has caused so much trouble. Now, I will have to bury him somewhere on the property, clean up the parlour, maybe throw away the table he decided to tarnish with his blood, and then I'll have to start from scratch again. Find someone who can keep up with my cravings, who can give me what I want. Until I do, I just hope Freddie has enough left in savings to get me through this tough time.

Sighing, I sit down on the empty chair and rub my temples. I need to think this through. Make sure I don't forget anything, leave no shred of evidence that can link me to Freddie's death. It would be best if no one ever found his corpse. No body, no crime, they always say.

I guess I have no choice but to call *her*. I'm too winded up to handle this on my own, and despite what she said last time we spoke, she'll help me. She has to. We're family.

I walk over to the phone in the hallway and call her number. Although it's been years, I still remember every digit. We were never particularly close, but she was there for me when it really mattered.

She picks up after the third ring. "Elizabeth Wakefield," my mother says from the other end of the line. "Who is this?"

I lick my lips, trying to speak, but the words die in my throat.

"Hello?" Mother says. "Who is this? If this is a prank call, I certainly don't—"

"It's me," I cut in, interrupting her.

She stays quiet for a moment. "It's been a while," she says eventually, a statement that holds a million thoughts and emotions, despite its simplicity.

I take a deep breath. "Mother, I…I need your help."

Another silence from the other end of the line. Just when I start to fear she will hang up on me, she speaks, "You've done it again, haven't you?"

I nod and then realise she will not be able to see my gesture. "Yes," I mutter into the telephone. No apologies, no excuses. She knows what kind of monster I am, and I know the monster she is; we're more alike than anyone will ever know.

"First your father, now your husband." Mother sighs. "You will have to find a way to control yourself, or this will never end. No one can give you *everything*."

No one can satisfy my desires, she means. I simply want too much. *Need* too much.

"I'll come over," Mother says. "We can't do the same we did with your father. Two burglary stories will raise suspicion. It's best if we just get rid of the body this time."

My Father's death. Covered up by a story involving burglars that never existed. I've tried to push that night to the back of my memories, but somehow, it always resurfaces, like a nasty itch that keeps begging to be scratched.

Mother gives me instructions, and like a good daughter, I listen to her every word. At the end of the call, I hang up and get to work.

I feel a thousand years old, exhausted to the bone, while I clean the floors until not a single drop of blood is left.

After I finish my task, I stand in the hallway, leaning against the doorframe and look at Freddie's body. I'm not sorry for what I did, but I do feel bad it had to end this way. In another life, we could've been happy. Maybe for someone else, his love alone would've been enough.

But not for me. For me, it will never be enough.

I'm a creature born from greed, a needy worm that always wants more and more, thriving on goods, and hoping these *things* can somehow make up for what I lack.

Love.

Need Can Be Satisfied

by Maxine Churchman

Ed and Charlie were flicking through a car magazine together when Ed's phone rang. The screen displayed Rob's name, his younger brother, and he hesitated over the reject button before answering the call.

He put it on speaker. "Hi Rob. You ok?"

There was a pause before Rob answered, "Yeh. You busy, I need some help?"

And there it was: the reason for his brother's call. Charlie raised her eyebrows.

Ed pinched the bridge of his nose and screwed his eyes shut. He was always bailing Rob out. He couldn't keep the exasperation from his voice. "What do you need?"

"No really, I can make it worth your while. I've got a job now."

"That's great, Rob. Congratulations." He smiled at Charlie, and she gave him the thumbs up.

"Yeh, I'm doing a house clearance right now, but my

partner dropped something heavy on his foot—silly prick was wearing sandals—he's gone for an x-ray. I just need a bit of help carrying some stuff. Can you come? I'm over in Newington."

Charlie nodded and mouthed, "We'll both go."

"Sure." They could do with some extra money—they were saving for a new car. "Charlie's here, we'll both help. We'll get a taxi; you can pay."

Twenty minutes later, they pulled up next to the removals lorry, and Rob paid the driver before giving Ed a slap on the back and a curt nod to Charlie. "Thanks for this."

They spent the next half hour hauling items from the house to the lorry. Charlie amused herself, peeking into boxes before carrying them out. When they had finished, only the light bulbs and permanent fixtures remained.

They drove the haul east, towards the outskirts of the city, and turned into a rundown district. It was not an area Ed was used to visiting. Small houses and shacks were crammed together. Scruffy children in ragged clothes played in the dirt at the side of the road, while skinny dogs slinked between piles of rubbish. Charlie stiffened and held his arm.

Elderly men and women sat outside their front doors. They smiled and waved as the lorry drove past. It was hard to believe that just a few streets over were the mansions of the wealthiest members of society, spread out amongst leafy landscaped grounds.

They pulled up outside a huge warehouse, where a group of men and women was unloading another lorry. Rob jumped down to open the back. More people emerged from the building and greeted Rob with cheerful grins.

Charlie grabbed Ed's arm as he was about to get out. "There is a box of jewellery in the back. It must be worth thousands. What are they going to do with it all?"

He shrugged. "Let's find out."

Above the entrance to the building hung a large painted sign that read "Here to satisfy your NEED—NOT your GREED."

"What is this place?" he asked Rob.

"It's the Need Not Greed project."

Ed shrugged; he'd not heard of it.

"Anyone who needs something they can't afford can take it from here." Rob smiled proudly and held his arm out towards the building. "Things of value, like jewellery, paintings—stuff you don't really need—and anything that has been here for a while, is auctioned or repurposed. The other end of this building opens into Bay Street, so those with plenty of spare cash don't have to see the unfortunates." He made air quotes as he said unfortunates. "All profits are ploughed back in. It provides jobs, schooling, and free stuff for the poor and disadvantaged."

Charlie picked up a box with a cross marked on it.

Rob touched the top. "Any boxes with a cross are for auction. It needs to go next to the red door at the far end of the room."

As Rob turned away, Charlie caught Ed's eye—he knew that look. She blew him a kiss and he watched her walk confidently towards the building, hoping she wouldn't get caught doing something stupid.

He helped Rob carry a large armchair over to the lounge furniture section, where there were already plenty of sofas and armchairs in various colours and sizes.

Rob grunted as they lowered it to the ground. "This will probably get auctioned or stripped down. It will be too big for most of the houses round here." He looked past Ed's shoulder. "That old fella looks like he needs some help. Can you carry on emptying the lorry? I'll be back as soon as…"

While Rob was helping the old man, Ed intercepted Charlie on her way back to the entrance. She looked pleased with herself.

"I put the box in that big blue wardrobe." She pointed towards the back of the room. "You can come back later and get the jewellery."

"Is that a good idea?"

"Look around, honey—there's loads of stuff. They won't miss one little box." She hooked her arm in his and rubbed her face against his shoulder, fluttering her eyelids. "You could sell it to Grayson—get some money for our dream car."

He had to admit—the idea had appeal.

He was still thinking about it as Rob drove them home. "So this project helps the poor and needy. Who decides who's in need?"

Rob frowned. "The needy decide for themselves."

Charlie snorted.

"I'm telling you; it works really well. The area was a hotbed of crime and violence before Phil Grover's project turned it all around. Phil should stand for philanthropist."

Ed curled his lip. "Phil Grover of Grover International? I thought he died." He'd heard some awful things about the company owned by Phil's father, Garth— fat tycoons getting rich by crushing the dreams of anyone who got in their way.

"The helicopter accident, you mean?" Rob asked.

Rumours circulated that it was no accident. "Yeh, I thought they both died, father and son."

Rob nodded. "Ground crew said he was aboard when

the chopper took off, but they didn't find his body. All a bit strange, but he turned up safe and well a few weeks later claiming some mumbo jumbo about being given a second chance."

Suspicious. Maybe Phil killed his father to take over the business. Not his worry, Garth was no great loss.

Rob glanced at him as if he could read his mind. "Phil's a good bloke. He restructured the business and rooted out the greed. He doesn't get the credit he deserves. People are only interested in gossip and intrigue."

Charlie was humming to herself; she'd lost interest, but Ed was still perplexed. "So the poor can access that building whenever they want and take anything they need?"

Rob stopped the lorry outside Ed's place. The brakes hissed like a tetchy teacher, fed up with explaining something over and over again. "Not just the poor. Anyone who needs—needs not wants mind—something they can't afford can get it from the warehouse. Dawn 'til dusk. Every day, even Christmas day."

Ed watched Charlie open their front door. "What stops them taking stuff to sell?"

Rob frowned. "Nothing, but it doesn't happen." He shrugged. "Superstition maybe—it's rumoured Phil has far-reaching powers since his dice with death."

Ed took their money and jumped down. His mind was in overdrive thinking about the possibilities. He watched Rob drive away.

Charlie handed him a rucksack from the hallway. "Go do your stuff before dusk."

He jumped in his beat-up car and was relieved when it started first time.

There were no vehicles outside when he arrived, but the doors were still open. A young boy, emerging with a table lamp, waved and grinned. His feet were bare; perhaps he should have got himself some shoes.

A pang of conscience made Ed's stomach clench as he re-read the sign. He almost lost his nerve, but the lure of a new car, and Charlie's ire, was too much to resist. Dammit! Charlie was right: they *needed* money for a new car.

Ed took the rucksack and headed straight for the wardrobe. There was no one about, but he wanted to get out before the doors were locked, so he just emptied everything from the box into the bag. As he made his way to the exit, he passed some cutlery. He picked up two each: knives, forks, and spoons. If anyone saw him leaving, the cutlery would detract from the bag on his back.

His eyes were drawn to the notice above the door—

he hadn't seen it earlier.

"Take only what you need—beware greed—your sins will find you out."

He shivered and quickly looked away, gritting his teeth. Outside a man sauntered towards the building swinging a ring of keys.

"Did you find everything you need?" he called out cheerfully.

Ed held up the cutlery. "Yes, thanks." He hastily opened the car door, chucked the bag onto the passenger seat, before sliding in and wiping the sweat from his brow. He drove away from the area and stopped in an empty carpark to make a call to Grayson.

Ten minutes later, he walked up a path between well-manicured lawns and knocked on a shiny mahogany door. Grayson ushered him inside and led him to a large airy kitchen.

Ed tipped everything onto the table and Grayson used a loop to scrutinise each piece, before placing them in piles. Ed drank coffee in silence as he watched him work. Some of the items looked expensive to his untrained eyes, and he felt his excitement grow.

When he'd finished, Grayson pushed one pile towards Ed. "These are just costume jewellery, virtually worthless, but I'll give you eighteen hundred for the rest."

Ed banged his cup down. "Is that all! I was hoping for at least three grand."

Grayson stared at him, his beady brown eyes behind the thick, horn-rimmed glasses were unblinking; but Ed kept his nerve and stared back, clenching his teeth, because it made him look hard.

Grayson looked away first. "Final offer—two and a half—including the costume."

Ed liked to have the final bid; he grabbed a gaudy necklace from among the costume jewellery and countered, "Ok, but I'm keeping this one."

They shook on the deal, and he left with a wad of notes, the necklace, and a feeling of great satisfaction. He was happier than he had been for a while.

At home, Charlie's eyes sparkled at the sight of the money.

He held up the necklace. "This isn't worth much, but I think it would look great on you." He walked behind her and fastened it round her neck. She touched the stones and looked in the mirror. He stood behind her. The blue stones, which resembled sapphires, matched her eyes perfectly and the chunky gold-coloured chain contrasted beautifully with her smooth pale skin. He kissed her neck.

She turned and smiled. "I think we should go back tomorrow and see what else we might need. At this rate, we'll have the car in no time."

Ed wasn't so sure: after all, wasn't it stealing? He dumped the cutlery in the sink on their way up to bed. He'd worry about it all in the morning.

Charlie removed her clothes seductively but kept the necklace on. He'd made a good choice, and he loved that Charlie was in such a good mood. Perhaps another trip to the project tomorrow was a good idea after all.

Ed woke. It was still dark. He was on his side facing away from Charlie. He smiled to himself—she'd been wild last night. He rolled onto his back and reached out for her. Her skin was cold and unyielding to his touch. He sat up and switched the bedside lamp on. Squinting against the sudden glare, he could see her lips were blue and there was a vivid purple line under the necklace round her neck. She was dead. He put his head in his hands, confused and upset, but he was distracted by a noise on the stairs: a metal clink. He held his breath listening; his eyes fixed on the door. Was someone in the house? Had they killed Charlie while he slept?

The sound came again: a clink and a scrape.

His heart hammered, he was afraid to move. He kept listening while he tried to remember where the wooden baseball bat was. He used to keep it under the bed, before he bought a divan. He turned his head and was relieved to see it in the corner.

The sound came again, closer now, possibly on the landing outside the door.

He scrambled out of bed, grabbed the bat, and faced the door again. Was it better to wait for the door to open or take the intruder by surprise? He was paralysed with indecision.

He jumped when something hit the door on the other side. It gave him the impetus to move behind the door, so he would be hidden if it opened. Sweat trickled down his face, tickling his nose. He wiped it away with the back of his hand. The handle of the door started to turn, slowly, so slowly. A scream built in his chest, and he swallowed it down. He wanted to grab the handle and yell in the intruder's face. Maybe he would be scared off—maybe he would be armed and kill him.

The door opened a crack. He gripped the handle of the bat harder, with both hands, until his knuckles turned white. A pain shot through his foot. He cried out in agony and dropped the bat. A fork was sticking in the side of his heel, the tines buried deep in the fleshy part. It was one he'd picked up at the project. He grabbed the handle and pulled it out, tears welling in his eyes. The fork started twisting in his hand and he nearly let it go. The shock made him step back, just as a knife skimmed past his nose and buried itself in the wall beside him, vibrating from the impact. He looked around wildly; where was the other knife and fork? The spoons beat a tattoo on the top of his head. Dazed, he fell to his knees, covering his head with his hands, just as the other knife whistled overhead and landed on the bed. He dived onto the knife and secured it, with the fork, in his right hand. They wriggled and twisted so much he had to use both hands. The spoons hit him on the head again, and he rolled onto the floor. He forced the knife and fork into a discarded sock, tied a knot in the top, and shut it in a drawer, while trying to keep out of the way of the spoons. They rapped his knuckles as he tried to catch them. The knife in the wall had almost wiggled free; he lunged for it and just as he grasped the handle, the other fork sank its tines into his right bicep. The knife fell to the floor and he stomped his foot on it quickly, holding it there as it twisted and wriggled. He managed to catch one of the spoons and was about to wrench the fork out of his arm when the other spoon started smacking the toes on the foot securing the knife. He grabbed both the spoon and the knife and wrapped them in a t-shirt. When he pulled the fork out, his arm bled alarmingly, but he secured the cutlery in the drawer before wrapping his arm tightly in a bandage from the bathroom.

At last, he sat exhausted on the edge of the bed. He looked at his phone. He needed to call the authorities, but how was he going to explain this? It would not look good. They would think he killed Charlie and she injured him trying to fend him off.

Who would believe a bunch of inanimate objects had punished them for their greed?

You Don't Want What I Get

by Michelle Ann King

The others don't like me. Partly because I'm a girl and partly because I don't like them either, but mostly because I'm treated differently.

When they go up to collect their cut, I stay where I am, sitting on the table. Smoking. They don't like that either, some of them. Bunch of tough guys worried about lung cancer. Crazy. I tell them I need the cigs for anger management purposes, and the boss backs me up. The boss gives me a lot of leeway, especially with my anger management issues. Something else they don't like.

You'd think they'd be pleased—wouldn't you—that I don't take anything out of the pot? Means more for them. But they don't think that way. They wonder what else it is that I'm getting. Wonder if it's something better. I suppose I shouldn't be surprised: paranoia and suspicion are survival tools in our line of work.

Richie's the first one to get into it. I thought he would be. He's young and impetuous. Insecure, too. It makes him front harder. I don't know if he's got a genuine problem with women or if that's just part of the show. All amounts to the same thing in the end, I guess.

He flicks his fingers at the money, like it's nothing, and plants himself in front of me. Folds his arms to make his biceps pop. I'm tempted to use one to stub out my smoke, but I don't. Escalation isn't classy at my age.

The other guys shuffle. Some want to see it go down, some just want it to go away. Professionalism, or just another age thing? Maybe that doesn't matter either.

"Take your money and go home, boy." That's Oz, who's been around a long time. Long enough not to ask questions.

Richie's not playing along. He's got a different script in his head, written a different ending.

"Fuck you, old man."

He carries on looking at me when he says it. Disrespectful. Any regret in Oz's face hardens out. Richie's strong, fast, skilled with a blade. He could have been useful. But he wants more than that. Wants too much, too soon. Sometimes it shakes out that way, with the good ones.

Oz shoots a look at the boss. That's the difference, right there. Oz knows what he wants, but he also knows that isn't what counts.

The boss looks Richie up and down. Kid doesn't even notice. How could you not feel that? But he's all about me. Getting closer, puffing up. He's got a foot and a half on me anyway, and that's without me sitting down. He's not quite big enough to do it on sheer physicality, but he's got the eyes, too. There's a look that sells it, and he's close. Another few kills—more measured, more deliberate—and he'd have it down.

Shame. I hate waste.

But maybe I'm being too quick to judge. Too eager to find Richie wanting. It's possible; I've been wrong before. Sometimes they surprise you.

Oz looks at the boss. The boss nods.

Oz looks at me. Shrugs.

What will be, will be.

I slide off the table. "Let's go," I tell Richie and head out the door.

For a moment I don't think he's going to follow, but he jogs down the hallway after me.

"So you don't like money?" I ask him. "You don't want to get paid?"

"I don't like getting cut out," he says. "There's something you got going on, and I want in."

"No, you don't," I say.

I stop, so that he runs into me. His upper chest hits

my shoulder.

He spins on the impact but keeps his feet. His eyes widen, and his hand goes to his chest before he jerks it back down again.

I wait. If he backs out now, I'll let him. The good ones know how to follow orders but the best ones know how to calculate and adapt. There's no shame in being beaten, only in not realising it.

But Richie's script has too deep a hold. I can see him process, assess, and dismiss in almost the same moment. Superiority bounces back into his face and stance like elastic.

So be it, then.

I walk on. He hesitates for a fraction of a second but again follows. We both take the stairs two at a time.

"Where you going, bitch?"

"To get my cut," I say. "You want, I'll split with you. Fifty-fifty."

"Hell yeah, I want. But maybe I'll say what the split's going to be."

I look back at him. "Maybe."

We hit the lower floor. When this was a real meat warehouse, it was cold storage. It's not so different now. Just not so cold.

The way Richie's looking around, I can tell he's

never been down here. He must have heard the rumours, though. Everyone has.

"What is this?" he says.

I key in the code for the inner door and open it up wide. "Files and Records."

He gags, his upper body spasming.

"Whew," I say. "Those files sure get ripe in the summer, don't they?"

He hangs back, one hand covering his mouth. A cloud of flies boils out from the back where the hooks are. Richie swats at them with his free hand. I stick out my tongue and let them land.

"What the fuck?" he says. Or at least, it sounds something like that.

He bends over and retches. I slip behind him and shut the door tight behind us.

"Jesus fuck," he says and pulls the knife out of his pocket. A switchblade. A bit dated, but still effective. In the right circumstances.

"You won't need that," I tell him. "Most of this is so tender by now, it'll slide right off the bone."

"Jesus fuck," he says again. "What the fuck is this?"

"Not that you want to neglect the bones." I yank an arm off the nearest hook and crunch on it. "They're an excellent source of calcium. Good for the teeth."

I show him mine, as proof.

He screams and scrambles backwards, his feet sliding on the floor. His back hits the door, and he holds out the switchblade in front of him. His hand is shaking so badly that it's just jittering up and down, but at least he tries. He hasn't pissed himself yet, either. Points. He might still come out the other side of this. I'd like that. He does have potential, after all.

I finish the arm and pull off a nice plump thigh. "Thing is, Richie, everyone knows when the job's been done and the books are balanced, and the boss doesn't really want to keep any files or records hanging around. He wants them gone. So his needs and my needs intersect quite nicely. We're a good team."

I step closer to Richie, and he drops the knife. "You wanted to be on my team, didn't you, Richie? You wanted to share?"

He closes his eyes and murmurs something. I think it might be a prayer.

I take a bite out of the leg and chuck the rest into his lap. "All yours," I say.

A Handful of Dead Leaves

by Alannah K. Pearson

The man hurried along the dark road. Oak trees clustered close, overhanging branches trying to block his path. He quickened his pace, casting furtive glances behind him at the shifting shadows. All knew the stories told at hearthside—warnings about the Fair Folk, the dangers of the woods after dark. But the harvests were poor, work not plentiful. He had no choice.

Suddenly, the wind gusted, spiralling leaves along the road. He pulled the thin felt coat tighter about his body, stuffing mitten-clad hands deeper into his pockets. Behind him, a twig snapped. He stopped, chest heaving with fearful gasps. Faint laughter echoed through the woods. He crossed himself, whispering a prayer. A fox barked from the nearby meadows. On the horizon, the sun was setting. He scanned the forest with wild eyes, shadows writhing among the oak trees.

He bolted down the road like a spooked horse. Around him, the woods erupted in a cacophony of squawking, screeching cries. But still he ran, fleeing the wildwoods and that faint, awful laughter of the fae. The oaks above his head shifted and groaned in the wind, branches bending, scratching at him. He darted and twisted, trying to avoid their twiggy grasp. Then he heard the clattering hooves upon the road. Fear slid down his spine and settled in his stomach. The headless rider of the Sidhe, the Dullahan, darker than midnight, bringer of destruction and madness. *Run, for surely your life depends upon it.*

He darted off the road and into the undergrowth. All knew the Dullahan never left the roads. He would be safe here until the spectre passed. He tore his coat free from the clinging branches, staring at the village lights just beyond the hawthorns. A faint track twisted through the bracken, away from the road and reaching oak trees.

He fled along the path, his breath hanging in frozen clouds before him. Leaping over lichen-covered logs and skirting mossy boulders, he focused on the village lights beyond the forest. Branches slapped at his face; fear still curdled in his veins, muddling his wits. He tripped, falling to his knees in a clearing. Sitting on his heels, chest heaving like bellows, he stared around him, noticing the large, irregular stones that marked the circle.

"A fine evening to you, Connor O'Malley."

The man jerked, staring in shock at a diminutive figure on a fallen log—a fae he swore had not been there a moment before.

"How do you know my name?"

"I know many things about you, Connor," he said, lighting his tiny pipe. He stared at the plume of blue smoke drifting upwards into the night sky. Finally, he smiled maliciously. "I know you labour long in the fields for others, yet cannot provide for your lovely new wife. I know this winter will be a hard one. And I know you fear for Catherine and your unborn son."

"This is devilry," he protested. "The wee folk are stories to frighten children."

"And yet," the little man said, spreading his hands in a helpless gesture. "Here I am. Am I the devil? You're no child and yet you fear me."

"I know better than to treat with your kind."

"I'm sure you do," the fae agreed, bright eyes sharp. "But you wouldn't make a bargain with me, would you?"

He shook his head.

The little man smiled cruelly. "Surely you do not wish your Catherine to suffer in this coming winter? To watch your newborn son starve?"

"No," Connor pleaded.

"I could make certain such a fate does not befall

them. I could offer you a way to always protect Catherine from poverty, famine, and the bitter bite of winter."

Connor fidgeted, plucking at the hem of his coat sleeve. The leprechaun, for Connor was certain this hedgerow fae was one of those despised folk, ignored him, critically inspecting a large toadstool.

"The wee folk never offer favours without something in exchange," Connor said. "Tell me what you seek in return."

The eyes of the leprechaun brightened with malicious glee. "A mortal child in exchange for a prosperous future is all I seek from you, Connor O'Malley."

"You want me to steal a child?"

The leprechaun turned a remorseless gaze on him. "Not just any child. I want your first-born son."

Connor's breath caught in his chest. He stared incredulously at the leprechaun. "Why offer salvation from famine only to give you my son? What good would riches do me then?"

The little man adjusted his ill-fitting jacket. "If you and Catherine survive and prosper, you will be blessed with other children. What is one child if you might have more?"

"Such an agreement would be madness."

The leprechaun puffed on his pipe again. "Will your Catherine still care for you when there is no coin to buy food? Or when no fire can ward against the winter chill? When she must watch her son starve? Can you live with the knowledge you could have prevented those things?"

"Please don't say such things."

"Then you agree to our bargain?"

"I," Connor began, staring in horror at the cruel little fae, "I have no choice but agree."

"Then our pact is made, Connor O'Malley."

The leprechaun's pronouncement echoed in the silence. Connor blinked in shock, staring at the empty space where the horrid fae had been, where now only the lingering odour of pungent pipe smoke remained. The little man had vanished.

Shivering, Connor turned and saw the cottage lights just beyond the hawthorn trees. He stumbled over the earthen fae mound and hurried for home, the leprechaun's vicious smirk a haunting memory.

The winter famine was as harsh as the leprechaun had promised. Connor watched with haunted eyes as the cold nights took many lives from the village, the old and very young stolen away on the icy winds. Connor worked the fields as his fellows in the village succumbed to illness and later starvation. But Connor and his wife always had baskets of vegetables, bread, and cheese long past when others in the village could provide for themselves. Each evening, Connor's eyes strayed to the hawthorn trees around the fae mound on the outskirts of the village, and he feared the birth of his child. But after two turnings of the seasons, Connor began to forget his fear and caution of the wee folk, wondering if that night in the woods was nothing but momentary madness.

Catherine and Connor startled awake. The wind blew against the house, rattling shutters, whistling through the eaves with an eerie cry. Predawn light, anaemic and grey, filtered through the open window, the lace curtains fluttering in the gusting wind. Catherine's gaze went immediately to the cradle in the corner of the room; her hand clutched her breast. Dread lodged in Connor's stomach as he climbed quickly from the bed. He had expected this for so long now, and yet he was unprepared for it. He grabbed a spluttering candle from the bedside and hurried to the cradle, already anticipating what he would find.

At first, he thought the cradle was empty. The covers appeared undisturbed, there was no sound from his son. *They returned for their promised boon,* he thought wretchedly. Connor lifted the candle higher, revealing on the white blankets a small, knitted toy. But the thing within the cradle was not his son. A cruel mockery had been placed on the smooth white blankets. Twiggy limbs bound together with vine, tiny bones of forest animals bound together to form a skeleton, bird beaks and hedgehog spines glittering in the candlelight. The woven head of bone and forest detritus rested upon the lace pillow Catherine had lovingly sewn, the protective charms decorating the hem now askew. Connor wanted to retch. Instead, he reached for the pillow then stopped, hand shaking.

Behind him, Catherine gasped, grabbing his arm. She stood in shock; a soft keening sound escaped her mouth; her lips drawn back in a hiss and she suffocated a wail. Carefully, Connor slid the pillow from beneath the awful mockery of a child. A small pouch lay beneath, woven from the finest furs and spiderweb. He picked it up, acorns dangling like strange decorations from the vine-woven ties. It was surprisingly heavy in his hand, the unmistakable clink of coin within. Catherine gave a shuddering groan, finally collapsing to the floor, strength failing her.

Still not speaking, Connor tipped four gold coins into the palm of his hand. Disgusted, he tossed the fae pouch into the cradle but away from the woven thing within. He stared at the gold in his hand. His heart felt like a dying thing; it flailed in his chest, beat once, then seemed to stop. Had he sold his son to the Fair Folk for four gold coins? That was not enough to keep them from the beggar's hedgerow. Already the villagers suspected some eldritch dealing, how else had he and Catherine survived the winter famines, prospered when so many starved, grown wealthy enough to buy the debts and lands of their fellows? Behind him, Catherine was silently mouthing her son's name, but soon enough her grief would turn to rage. Soon enough, she would direct the blame to him.

He could not let her know the truth of what he had done. And yet, the sacrifice of their son had kept them alive. Surely, she would understand that. Without the aid from the wee folk, they would have starved with the rest of the village. He would make sure she understood why he had agreed to the leprechaun's offer.

Connor knelt, grasping Catherine's arms, and lifted her up beside him.

"What have you done?" she cried over and again.

"It was to save us."

Catherine's sobs became wails, and she beat her fists against his chest. He held her, taking the blows of anger and despair. He deserved them, but he knew she would come to accept the loss of her son. Connor understood he had deceived Catherine by not telling her, but she had been complicit in her self-deceit; never once had she wondered about their good fortune and where their prosperity had come from.

Connor put the gold coins into his trouser pocket and waited for Catherine's sorrow to ease. When at last, pale sunlight of mid-morning streamed through the open shutters, Connor tucked his wife into the bedcovers. He walked quickly to the window and closed the shutters, glancing down at the cradle as he did. Despite his irrational hope, the cradle was still empty. He picked up the fae pouch, surprised to find the weight and clink of gold returned to it. Frowning, he upended the contents. Another four coins rolled lazily across the floorboards. Connor's hands shook with something akin to excitement as he took the coins within his pocket, stacking them on the floor beside the cradle. He stared at them and then at the other four coins scattered across the floorboards.

"I hope one day you will understand the sacrifice made," Connor said to the unmoving form of his wife huddled in the bed.

When Catherine did not speak, Connor bent to retrieve the eight gold coins, dropping them into his pocket. He glanced at the fae pouch and quickly took it before leaving the room.

"My mother used to say the sea carried away sorrows," Catherine said, looking at the drizzle falling across the mountains behind the house. "I wish we could have left these lands and moved to the seaside."

"She was right about many things." Connor grimaced. "But you know why we can't leave these lands."

Catherine turned, watching her husband frown as the waistcoat buttons strained around his belly when he shifted on the settee.

"The doctor told you to be careful of indulgences lest the gout return," she chided him.

He waved her concerns away, pushing his slightly swollen feet into the long boots and standing up. Like many things about Connor, evidence of his greed and consumption of their fortune became more obvious each day.

"When will you return?" she asked.

"Not until after midnight."

Catherine regarded her husband as he stood with one hand on the latch of the heavy front door, top hat in his other hand.

"Stay away from the fae mound," he warned and, not waiting for her response, stepped out into the night.

"We always do," she said, the door closing on her words.

Catherine did not watch her husband leave nor wave him farewell from the cottage steps like she might have done many years ago. She had loved him once until that night when he returned home from the wood; fearful glances always cast towards the hawthorn trees surrounding the old mound. He had never told her of the bargain he had struck with that wretched hedgerow fae, not a word until the morning their son was taken by the wee folk. They had been blessed since then with prosperity and wealth. Connor owned more than half the lands around the village and more than half the debts for business within the township itself. Catherine had been blessed with four healthy children, not a serious injury or fever among them, but the shadow of her husband's betrayal still hung about their marriage. It did not matter what gowns or gifts he bestowed upon her—she knew their fortune was bought with the leprechaun gold Connor carried on his belt, the fae pouch he would never part with.

Yet when Connor was not here, Catherine often looked to the fae mound ringed by its hawthorns and felt a longing for the son she had lost.

The sudden laughter of her children drew Catherine outside into the warm night air. Her two eldest chased fireflies about the garden, their whoops of joy echoing in the silence. She sat in the wrought-iron chair, head tilted back to gaze at the night sky—the perfect starry dome above—and she frowned at a strange sensation humming through the garden like a plucked cello string.

Opening her eyes, she looked towards the hunched form of the earthen mound. There was a light moving between the hawthorns. *Shepherds searching for lost sheep?* She frowned, knowing the local shepherds refused to pasture their flock near the mound. They would not dare walk among the hawthorns on a Midsummer's Eve, not for an entire lost flock.

Catherine watched as a tall youth walked across the fields towards them, lantern held high in one hand. She could only stare at the boy. He would be nearly twenty years now, but his limbs were still lithe and supple like any youth and his curling black hair the same as Connor's, but his eyes were her own.

Catherine met the blue gaze and knew her eldest son. She took the hands of her younger children, entranced by the appearance of her son all these years since the wee folk had stolen him. He did not speak at all but waited with the lantern to illuminate their passage and Catherine followed, her other children trailing behind as they stepped beyond the hawthorn trees, the wooden garden gate sighing in the breeze.

The half-moon hung low above the fields as Connor walked up the estate drive. The servants were long gone to bed and Connor stalking inside to an oddly quiet house. The fireplace was stoked for the evening, but the rear doors onto the garden patio were wide open. Cursing Catherine's forgetfulness, Connor peered outside, noticing the children's toys were discarded around the patio. Annoyance warred with dread as he surveyed the eerily silent garden. No crickets, frogs, nor night birds, only a terrible sense of absence hung about the garden. Suddenly, a breeze blew the wooden gate at the far end of the garden. It squeaked loudly in protest. Connor's heart thudded. The gate was always kept latched.

Beyond the gate were the open fields and the fae mound, hunched and partially hidden amid the hawthorns. Catherine would never go near the mound; she'd never let the children play near it. Connor turned to admire the stone cottage and extent of his estates. Unconsciously, he reached for the fae pouch on his belt, its presence reassuring the agreement with the leprechaun was unbroken.

Connor's shaking fingers touched the soft fur of the pouch, some of the tension leaving him. He flexed his fingers, wanting to feel the familiar cold touch of gold beyond the fur. The contents of the pouch crackled loudly. He froze. Hurriedly, he pulled the vine-woven threads apart, fingers shaking so badly he fumbled with the opening of the bag.

He stared. The gold coins were gone. Mocking laughter seemed to come from the shadows surrounding the garden. Connor stared wildly around, searching for the source of the torment, but he could see no one. He felt for his pockets, hoping for the familiar touch of cold metal. His fingertips gave rise to another sharp crackle, and he withdrew his hand. The leprechaun's laughter echoed in the garden as Connor stared at his handful of dead oak leaves where once there had been gold.

Taker

by Nicola Currie

"All of it? What do you mean, all of it? That wasn't the deal."

I've done this so many times now but I still struggle to keep a straight face. The look of panicked incredulity on their faces when I tell them is so pathetic, it's hilarious. I should feel sorry for them but it's difficult when they bring it on themselves, with their own greed and stupidity. I mean, how can anyone want £500 so desperately they're willing to let someone cut a chunk out of their body, however small they think it will be? Get a job, idiot.

You're supposed to read the small print, stupid, I want to reply, but I keep things professional.

"I know this is difficult news, Adam," I say, my handsome trustworthy face wearing its best mask of sympathy, as I reflect his lost and devastated gaze in my own wide, concerned eyes. "As I mentioned when we discussed the risks of the procedure, complications are rare but not unheard of. Unfortunately, you are one of the unlucky few."

"A few cells, you said. A few cells."

He's barely into his twenties—an athlete, a clean eater, non-smoker—with every system in his body operating in peak condition. He's a walking fleshbag of precious gems as far as I'm concerned, each of his perfect organs glistening rubies. It's a shame I could only get him to agree to the kidney. I'd take it all if I could but I need the paperwork, just in case.

"A few cells," he continues. "For research purposes, to grow organs in your lab. You said I would be saving people. So you take my whole fucking kidney?"

It was a nifty little idea of mine, this particular con. Before, I was just another overworked doctor, making money on the side writing dodgy scripts for junkies who hadn't yet tripped away all of their dough. But when articles started to appear in the news about research into growing organs from stem cells, it was surprising how many people would come into my clinic thinking growing organs for human transplantation was already possible. Once it is on the Internet, idiots will believe it, I figured. Despite how right I was, not even I could have imagined what a gold mine it would turn out to be. It was easy to sucker people in. A tiny sample to save the life of another, I told them—a tiny operation. You'll be back on your feet with £500 in your pocket within two hours. Once they're in my operating room? Once they've woken back up afterwards? Oops, sorry!

"We had no choice," I say, my face grimaced into its best apology. "You suffered a highly unusual amount of bleeding. We did everything we could but it isn't something we could have foreseen."

"So what the fuck are you going to do about this?" The guy is starting to get agitated, shifting in his recovery bed like he is getting ready to come at me, until I see him wince and blanch from the pain.

"Our counsellors will be available to you for as long as you should need them. We'll also contact your general physician, who will be best placed to support you should you need any further care, though…"

"I'm talking about money, bitch. I want £2 million and a fast-track kidney transplant whenever I need one…"

This is the bit I secretly love. It's perverse I know, but it's a life-affirming realisation: They gave up so much to get so little, while quite the reverse is true for me. It reminds me that I'm a winner and all the spoils of life are waiting for me to take them.

"As a research charity, we are not in a position to hand anyone that kind of money. We, of course, want to recognise the anguish this has caused and as such will raise your payment to £3000 as a gesture of goodwill."

The guy laughs and then instantly regrets it, the

grimace returning to his face almost instantly.

"£3000? Is that a joke? I could sue you."

I watch his face fall as I explain how things are, show him the clause buried in the contract. Out loud, my words are gentle, contrite, but in my head I'm laughing, telling this loser to suck it. It's £3000 or nothing buddy, take it or leave it.

I see the hard glare of revenge fossilise in his ice-blue eyes as he signs the release paper I put in front of him, but I don't give even the smallest shit. As soon as I have the release from him, I get out of there, jump into my Aston Martin, and speed away. In a few days' time, once the last patient has been released, it will only take a few hours for my crew to tidy up the place. Should anyone come looking, it will look like the clinic was never even there.

When I get back to my hotel, champagne on ice is already waiting in my penthouse suite. I raise a toast to…what was his name?… Alan?…no, Adam, and the rest of the day's generous donors. Adam alone earned me a cool £1.2 million. It's hilarious. It isn't even that hard. All it takes is a fit young idiot, a rich desperate old guy, and a little introduction from me. Adam's kidney, meet desperate tycoon. Desperate tycoon, meet idiot's kidney.

I finish ordering dinner and a couple of women for the night, as my phone rings.

"Evening, boss."

Mike is my second in command, leading teams dismantling old clinics and setting up new ones so we can hop from city to city, entering quietly and moving out quickly, considerably richer than when we arrive. We go way back. He was actually my competitor once. While I dealt prescriptions from the comfort of my office, he lurked in alleys with prostitutes and criminals, dealing on the streets. He took issue with me at first, when I took my share of the market but saw the opportunity when I approached him with a new venture. A low life with a chequered past maybe, but he's always known how to get things done. Besides, it could come in handy one day, keeping someone like him around. *It wasn't my fault officer,* I'll tell the cops, looking as squeaky clean as my non-existence criminal record. *He made me do it,* I'll say, *I've been so scared. He spent three years in jail for beating someone into a wheelchair once, you know, officer.*

"Is everything ready for my arrival tomorrow?"

"Everything's taken care of. You've got seven pre-op consultations ahead of surgery over the next few days—two kidneys, a liver lobe, two lungs, and two eyes. The rest of the surgical team will follow behind you, arriving tomorrow evening, ready for the first surgeries the next day. The penthouse at the Central Spa Hotel is booked for you, too."

"Ok, but make sure you remember to ask for the hypoallergenic pillows this time. It pisses me off when you forget. And you need to start planning for our next target cities. All I've heard all day is how excited everyone is for the two-week break we're having after this next job, and it was so annoying. I regret letting you convince me with that wellness and personal time bullshit you keep spouting at me. Do you know what's good for my wellness? Making fucking money! So you'd better have some big plans for when we're all back from our pointless little holidays. I expect growth, in both donors and profits, to make up for the wasted time. So hit me with it."

"Well..." I'm not sure if Mike is hesitant or distracted by the screeching interference that wails down the line for a second. "Shit, sorry, just walked past the hotel's power supply cupboard I think. The thing is, boss, I think we need to take a break that's longer than two weeks. Six months or so, to reassess, restrategise. Maybe now's a good time to get out."

I can't believe what this fucking idiot is saying to me. Get out? We've barely fucking begun.

"What the fuck are you talking about? Do you know

how much money I made this week? Over six million, after costs. Ten percent of that is yours, don't forget. Why would you want to walk away from what could be a billion-dollar opportunity with a little more time? We should be branching out, building additional teams all around the world, not pussying out!"

"But we can't control something that big—they'll be too many of them."

"Too many what?"

"Victims."

I let the line fall silent for a moment but can't help myself. I laugh. I thought Mike had more sense than this.

"Victims? They're not victims. Do you think for one second any one of them gives a shit about donating to save someone else's life, even if they do think it is only a few cells? All they see is the opportunity to make a quick buck. If they want to be greedy and stupid, it's not my fucking fault if they don't consider the risks properly."

"But they'll still talk. It's inevitable they'll start to figure it out once more and more vic…donors come forward. We need an exit plan."

The truth is I already have one. I have for some time. Like I said, Mike is the perfect fall guy. I've already made all the arrangements I need to but the tricky part is when. I was going to stop at £10 million, then 25, 50. Now I'm close to 100, I keep telling myself that is it but…it still doesn't feel like enough.

But I can't let on to Mike. He can't bolt before I do.

"Ok, Mike, I see what this is. Negotiation. Fair play. You're a businessman, like me, I get it. How about we start talking real money. If you can expand the business like I want you to, I guarantee you two mil a week. How does that sound?"

The line is quiet for a moment, tense. I can imagine his excited heart beating, wanting to commit but too afraid to go all in. I wish he wasn't such a fucking loser.

"I'm interested, of course. But is there any way we can go legit? I heard about this company that can actually grow organs now and…"

"Are you fucking serious? We're not a fucking charity. I don't care if some virgin research scientist somewhere has figured out he can grow you a new arsehole in the morning and have you ready to shit by lunchtime. Our business is money and why pay for our raw resources when we can get them for free?"

"Because we're maiming people, boss! Even killing some of them…"

"Oh, there's only been like a dozen deaths and that was at the beginning, while I perfected things. And I knew nobody would miss them. That's why I chose homeless guys."

"But what if someone finds the bodies?"

"What do you mean finds the bodies? Earth to Mike, come in Mike? You know as well as I do that I paid off a crematorium to destroy the bodies. What is up with you?"

"Sorry, boss," Mike said, with a weird sigh of relief, like he really did forget what we did with the bodies. "I just had a wobble. You're right. This could be huge."

"Stick with me, Mike, and I'll make you so rich, we might kill a thousand people and still nobody'll touch us."

I hear the smile in Mike's voice as he finally agrees to get to work on future clinics and hangs up.

With perfect timing, my whores arrive. They are gorgeous and immaculately dressed. I see their eyes light up as they take in the room and I offer them champagne. With any transaction, I make sure to set expectations from the outset.

"Let me be clear, ladies. If you want a tip, I expect you to earn it."

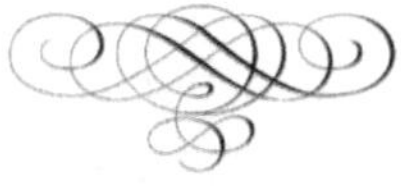

Late next morning, I eat a good breakfast and shower before heading out. The next city is less than 150 miles away so for once, I've decided to drive down, enjoy my Aston.

What the fuck is your problem, mate? The guy in the shitty Micra behind me is driving too fast. I change lanes to let him overtake but he moves with me. He tailgates me for several minutes, until I jolt forward. The prick rammed me! I glare into the rear-view mirror. When I see the ice-blue eyes glaring back at me, I realise. My last donor. Adam. And he is very pissed off.

He rams me again and I'd laugh if I wasn't so incensed. Does he really think he has a chance with his shitty Micra? I flip him off and accelerate hard. Almost immediately, he is as insignificant in the distance as he should be.

What a loser for thinking…

Suddenly, I am shot with fragments of glass as my car explodes from the passenger side. The sound of a loud horn is the last thing I hear before everything turns black.

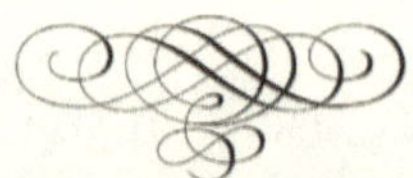

If I wasn't in so much pain, I'd laugh at life's irony. As I lie in bed, I almost sympathise with Adam and his kind. This sucks. My whole body is sore but particularly my back. They had to remove my kidneys. They were crushed beyond repair as my car flipped into a spin after its collision with an articulated lorry. Still, so much of me aches. I want to get a good look at my body, assess it for myself, as soon as they remove the bandages from my eyes.

"You're sure this is the best hospital around here?" I ask Mike again.

"Definitely, boss, definitely," he says. "And it's such a coincidence, too. It's owned by that company, the one that says they can actually grow organs. That lorry must have been fate."

I don't like coincidences. Coincidences are more often than not the sign of a con. Still, if there is any truth in what Mike is telling me, I'm a lucky boy, given my sudden need.

"How easy do you think it'll be to get two new kidneys grown?"

"You'll find that out for yourself soon enough," a new voice, a lady, says entering the room. I hear Mike laugh and something about it makes me nervous.

"Who's that?" I ask. I hear footsteps as someone moves around to the side of my bed.

"I'm Doctor Collins," the lady says. "But from now on, how about you call me boss?" I feel her unwind the bandages, but she stops halfway, my field of vision reduced to its right side.

"Who the fuck are you? And why have you stopped? Take the rest of these bandages off."

Her pretty eyes open in mock surprise. Mike is smirking despite the cuffs around his wrists and the two officers that guard the door.

"But they are off."

I try to understand what she means, why I can only see from one eye. She hands me a mirror. I scream.

Where my left eye was there is now only a bloody socket.

"Why didn't you tell me I lost an eye in the accident?"

"Because you didn't," Dr Collins says. "Truth be told, you didn't lose your kidneys in the accident either. We took those afterwards, along with your stomach, part of your liver, your small bowel, a lung, and a testicle. Don't look so upset. Let's none of us pretend you don't deserve it."

Mike is smirking at me, his eyes lit up with a dark victory.

"What the fuck have you done, Mike? Why?"

"Why?" Mike spits. "Why? It was bad enough when you stole my customers, when you left me no option but to work for you as your full-time bitch. But then I find fake documents, fake emails, fake accounts, all created by you, ready to set me up as soon as things got too hot. So when the authorities caught on to us, you can't blame me.

They were looking for a real scumbag, who deserved it, who no one could defend. So I gave them you."

"What authorities?" I panic as I feel for my balls and confirm what they say is true, my breath laboured as I start to hyperventilate. "What the fuck do they want with me?"

Dr Collins strokes my head.

"Hush, now. We can't have you overexerting yourself. We need you. You're our host. The perfect host. We've been trying to get this project approved for years but there were ethical concerns. What would the public say if they realised the government had approved a human study as cruel as this, however noble the cause? When we identified you, with the help of Mike here in exchange for a reduced sentence, and the approval board heard of everything you had done, well...they were not so concerned about ethical treatment any longer."

"So you're going to take my organs out, one by one, to give to someone else? That's sick, that's—"

"Exactly what you have been doing," Dr Collins says coldly. "But that's not our plan. We believe we can use you for something much more exciting, something that means you'll be able to pay back every one of the organs you stole. We *can* grow organs, you see. But we need a host body. It is very painful to grow a new organ and to grow several, over and over again—well, it's nothing short of torture. Still, no one seems to mind now that body will be yours. You can take the other one, gentlemen."

"Have a nice life," Mike smirks as the heavies lead him away. "Boss."

I try to scream, to sit up, but I am weak. I hurt.

"Quiet now," Dr Collins says, clicking out the light as she leaves behind them. "If you're a good boy, I'll buy you little treats every now and again. Your bank accounts have been cleared, by the way. All of your victims will find themselves winning the lottery or cash prizes for competitions they don't even remember entering over the next few months. Karma's a funny thing, isn't it?"

Commodity Items

by S.O. Green

"It's the heist of a lifetime," Harley told her. Which made five so far in Jan's lifetime.

"Oh really?" she asked, feigning interest as best she could. "Tell me more."

She leaned back against the bar while he obliged and told her about the prison and the shady fuck who'd moved in. About the mountains and mountains of provisions he'd hoarded there, filling up the cells like they were his personal larder. About how easy it would be to fill up a truck and ride out with more shit than they could feasibly ever use if only they could crack the automated security.

"That's where you come in," he said, and that was the punchline she'd been waiting on because—come on—it was *Harley*.

They had very specific skillsets. Harley's brand had been built on punching people, looming menacingly, and toting a sawn-off shotgun. He was a one-trick pony, but he did his trick very well. He had neither the patience nor the forehead slope for working with machines and that, as Harley had so succinctly put it, was where Jan came in.

She didn't have the shoulders for punching, the height for looming, or the shotgun for toting. What she did have was an array of knives (sharp), a black fauxhawk (roots showing), and a knack of making computers do what she wanted, when she wanted, how she wanted, for the reasons that most appealed to her.

"So, we crack security and then…"

"And then nothing. The guy's a paranoid idiot. Won't let another human being within a hundred fucking yards of the place. Shut down his automata and that's it. Game over. Wrap him up in duct tape and steal his shit."

"Seriously? He doesn't have a single, living soul in that prison with him?"

"Damn straight. That's why it's easy money. Any other target, we're looking at five, maybe six, guys to split the take with. For this, all we'll need is two."

He waggled the requisite fingers at her, though one was missing a digit. A raider gang had cut it off after they'd caught him cheating at cards. They'd made him eat it.

"Who's your source?" she asked. Code and life were both about the details.

"A friend."

"A friend who knows a guy whose cousin told him?"

"Just a friend. Seriously, the info's good. Trust me."

"You don't ask much, do you, Harl?"

"Nah. I usually don't bother asking. But I like you." He leaned in, grinning, giving her the full benefit of the stale beer smell on his breath. "I heard he's got meds in there, Jan. That'd help, right?"

She scowled and rode out the wave of sudden regret at spilling her deepest, darkest secrets to him one drunken night. Why she paid for that hotel room she never slept in, full room and board, constantly slipping letters and packets to the concierge and getting misty over the thought of what lay on the bed and coughed away its nights, entombed there.

Everyone had their price. She knew Harley's. She supposed it was only right that he knew hers.

"Alright," she said, with a bitter smirk, and she lifted her beer so they could make it final. "Let's rob the dickhead."

The prison had held five hundred people once. Super maximum. Impenetrable. Augmented by the new Warden and his army of automata, which patrolled the perimeter, walked the walls, and hovered over the compound on shimmering jets of superheated air.

Jan watched a tank bot rumble past, turning the

already obliterated foliage into mulch under its treads. Never deviating from its programming. Infrared eyes swept the darkness. Scanning, processing, interpreting. Its laser cannon and Gatling gun were both less than encouraging.

"You're one hundred percent sure he doesn't have anyone else in that building with him?"

"Jan, look at that fucking place. Why would he need people? You have to *pay* people. You have to *feed* them. And sometimes they get greedy."

She laughed. Case in point, here were two more greedy fuckers about to show the Warden why he was better off with machines.

"So, can you do it?" Harley asked.

"Who do you think you're talking to?"

Harley never slept in a cold bed, and Jan had never met a computer whose pants she couldn't infiltrate. Same principles. The confidence of your proposal and a deep understanding of what they *really* wanted.

Passwords were shallow. Biometrics? Lip service! Machines didn't want your words or to gaze into your eyes. They wanted to know you in their heart and soul. Their code. Touch that and you opened up a world of possibilities.

A world where the tank bots stopped rolling and the

lights dimmed in the bipeds' eyes and the drones returned to their charging stations for a little shut-eye. Jan kissed them all goodnight and slipped her tablet into her hip pouch.

"Nap time," she said.

"Alright." Harley toted his shotgun. "Time to get what we came for."

They found the Warden in, of all places, the Warden's office. He was sleeping on an iron cot with a single blanket. Sparser than she'd expected for a man with a building full of all sorts of everything.

Harley slapped him awake with a "rise and shine, you piece of shit," flashed his shotgun, loomed a little, and punched him in the stomach so that he knew what he'd get if he stepped out of line. Jan stood in the door and wondered if Harley wouldn't have fit right in at that prison, either as an inmate or a guard.

They dragged the Warden down into his larder. He was silent. Sullen. He'd put his faith in machines, and the machines had betrayed him just as surely as men would have, all because someone else had understood them better than he had. Jan didn't give a shit about irony and Harley didn't understand it, so the poetry was lost on all of them.

He was a neat man, tall, and well-built. Not burly like one of his captors, nor runty like the other. He wore clean, neutral colours, and Jan wondered where he'd found them in this crumbling world. What little he said betrayed efficiency and intellect and an absolute lack of preparedness for this eventuality.

They found his stores in the cells. He'd organised and catalogued everything meticulously. Tinned beans: 101. Tinned vegetables: 102. Tinned meat: 103. The list was endless. Harley leered at the bounty while Jan flipped through pages and pages of inventory.

"You've got *five cells* full of toilet roll?"

The Warden shrugged.

This was his dragon hoard. As good as gold. A currency for every nation. If everyone had a price, he had the payment. His automata had carved a swathe through the state, emptying stores, plundering bunkers. Burning settlements. All to fill this trove.

Harley kept the Warden on his knees, shotgun aimed at the back of his head. His composure was admirable, Jan supposed. She listened to them talk as she went exploring. Their voices carried in the concrete corridors.

"This is a lot of stuff," her partner said.

"Indeed. Enough to share between the three of us,

wouldn't you agree?"

"I ain't too good at math, but I'm pretty sure it's better to divide by two than three."

"I couldn't agree more."

Apprehension trickled down Jan's spine. The sudden realisation that she wasn't exactly sure how loyal someone like Harley could be. Then she heard him laughing.

"Nice try, asshole."

Bolstered, Jan pressed deeper. She passed a sign for the showers. There were lights on down here. A waste of power. Unless there was something to see.

"What the hell were you planning on doing with all this shit anyway?" Harley's echo asked.

"These are commodity items, my friend. Tradeable goods. The old systems of power have crumbled. Now, those who provide are the ones who prosper."

"You've got all this. What could anyone offer you?"

"Whatever I want."

There was a barred gate ahead. Old-fashioned key lock. No electronic panel. Her careless foot kicked a bucket lying in the corridor and it rattled away. Somewhere ahead, something gasped.

Jan walked to the gate. She peered through. Her heart quickened. Something hot started to bubble in her stomach.

Rage.

"Hey, Jan. What's—"

It was all Harley managed to say before she had the Warden on his back and one of those sharp knives under his chin. Blood ran thick onto her fingers and he cringed away, eyes beseeching her partner for clemency.

"Jan, what the fuck—?"

"Keys!" she snarled. "I want fucking keys!"

The Warden, balanced literally on a knife edge, told her about the desk in the security station and the bundle of old iron keys in the drawer. Harley was bewildered but still cooperative. He fetched them for her, held them up, and jangled them in far too cheerful a way considering what they unlocked.

"We can discuss this," the Warden pointed out.

"No," she said and stabbed him in the stomach. "We can't."

She stabbed him a few more times because the heat was still there. She stopped when she started to feel cold. She stood back, quivering. She'd left the knife between his ribs. His blood was on her hands.

"Holy shit, girl," Harley grunted. "I take back every bad thing I ever said to you."

She glared at him. She wasn't so unreasonable as to

knife a man for no reason. Or even a small reason.

She took the keys in her bloody hand and marched back into the maze. Harley followed, confused, because he was missing a pertinent piece of information.

She led him to the barred gate, found the right key, unlocked the door, and rolled it aside.

Then she kneeled down and said, "It's okay. You can come out now."

The first one was twelve. A blonde wearing a coverall that had never been meant for a child. The others ranged from four to fourteen. Scared, dirty, trembling, clinging to one another. Ten, twenty, thirty of them. They gathered before Jan and Harley, wide-eyed and whimpering.

Harley hid the shotgun and slid to his knees, because none of his skills seemed particularly useful right at that moment.

Jan looked back at him, eyes as sharp and red as the knife she'd left in the Warden.

"Commodity items," she spat.

Author Biographies

ALANNAH K. PEARSON

Alannah K. Pearson is a speculative fiction author, combining her interests and expertise in archaeology and ancient history, global folktales, mythologies and environment. Alannah's writing interests include Amerindian folktales, Norse mythology, Prehistory, Archaeology, Ancient History and Gothic folklore. Alannah also has an academic background in Archaeology, Prehistory and human evolution. When not writing, Alannah is completing a PhD in human and primate evolution or enjoying the Australian wilderness with two dogs (canine assistants). She is a keen nature and wildlife photographer, bookshop and Museum devotee. She lives in Canberra, Australia.

Website:www.alannahkpearson.com
Twitter: @AlannahKPearson

CHISTO HEALY

Chisto Healy has been writing since childhood, but he only started following his dreams and writing full time in 2020. On top of the award nominated self published novels from his earlier days, he now has 75 published stories. You can find out what is out to read at his blog or follow him on Amazon as there is new stuff constantly coming out. He lives in NC with his fiance and her mom, his daughter Ella who has inspired stories that have been published, and his daughter Julia who has been published alongside him, and his son Boe who thinks the world is his drum.

Blog https://chistohealy.blogspot.com

DAVID GREEN

David Green is a writer based in Co Galway, Ireland. Growing up between there and Manchester, UK meant David rarely saw sunlight in his childhood, which has no doubt had an effect on his dark writings. Published in places such as Nymphs, Nocturnal Sires and previous Black Hare Press anthologies, David is aiming to release his debut novel in 2020.

Twitter: @David Green
Website: davidgreenwritercom.wordpress.com

DAWN DEBRAAL

Dawn DeBraal lives in rural Wisconsin with her husband Red, two rat terriers, and a cat. She has discovered that her love of telling a good story can be written. Published stories with Palm-sized press, Spillwords, Mercurial Stories, Potato Soup Journal, Edify Fiction, Zimbell House Publishing, Clarendon House Publishing, Blood Song Books, Black Hare Press, Fantasia Divinity, Cafelit, Reanimated Writers, Guilty Pleasures, Unholy Trinity, The World of Myth, Dastaan World, Vamp Cat, Runcible Spoon, Dark Christmas, Siren's Call, Iron Horse Publishing, Falling Star Magazine 2019 Pushcart Nominee.

Amazon: amazon.com/Dawn-DeBraal/e/B07STL8DLX

DAWN KNOX

Dawn enjoys writing in different genres and has had romances, speculative fiction, sci-fi, humorous and women's fiction published in magazines, anthologies and books. She's also had two plays about World War One performed internationally. Her newest published book is 'The Basilwade Chronicles'.

Website: dawnknox.com
Twitter: SunriseCalls

EDDIE D. MOORE

Eddie D. Moore travels hundreds of hours a year, and he fills that time by listening to audiobooks. When he isn't playing with his grandchildren, he writes his own stories. You can find a list of his publications on his blog or by visiting his Amazon Author Page. While you're there, be sure to pick up a copy of his mini-anthology Misfits & Oddities.

Website: eddiedmoore.wordpress.com
Amazon: amazon.com/author/eddiedmoore

ERIK HANDY

Erik Handy grew up on a steady diet of professional wrestling, bad horror movies that went straight to video, and comic books. There were also a lot of video games thrown in the mix. He currently absorbs silence and fish tacos. In his spare time, he works a full-time job he hates.

Website: ErikHandy.com

G. ALLEN WILBANKS

G. Allen Wilbanks is a member of the Horror Writers Association (HWA) and has published over 100 short stories in various magazines and on-line venues. He is the author of two short story collections, and the novel, When Darkness Comes.

Website: www.gallenwilbanks.com
Blog: DeepDarkThoughts.com

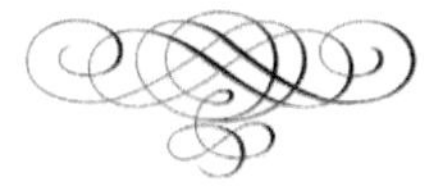

GABRIELLA BALCOM

Gabriella Balcom lives in Texas with her family, loves reading and writing, and thinks she was born with a book in her hands. She works in a mental health field, and writes fantasy, horror/thriller, romance, children's stories, and sci-fi. She likes travelling, music, good shows, photography, history, interesting tales, and animals. Gabriella says she's a sucker for a great story and loves forests, mountains, and back roads which might lead who knows where. She has a weakness for lasagne, garlic bread, tacos, cheese, and chocolate, but not necessarily in that order.

Facebook: GabriellaBalcom.lonestarauthor

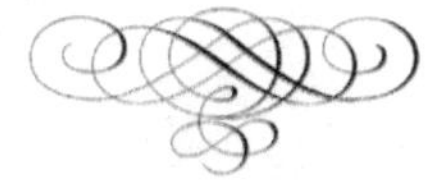

GALINA TREFIL

Galina Trefil is a novelist specialising in women's, minority, and disabled rights. Her favourite genres are horror, thriller, and historical fiction. Her short stories and articles have appeared in Neurology Now, UnBound Emagazine, The Guardian, Tikkun, Romea.CZ, Jewcy, Jewrotica, Telegram Magazine, Ink Drift Magazine, The Dissident Voice, Open Road Review, and the anthologies "Flock: The Journey", "First Love", "Sea of Secrets", "Coffins and Dragons", "Organic Ink Volume One", "Winds of Despair", "Waters of Destruction", "Curses & Cauldrons", "Unravel", "Hate", "Love", "Oceans", "Forgotten Ones", "Dark Valentine Holiday Horror Collection", and "Suspense Unimagined".

Website: galinatrefil.wordpress.com
Facebook: Rabbi-Galina-Trefil-535886443115467

HARI NAVARRO

Hari Navarro has, for many years now, been locked in his neighbours cellar. He survives due to an intravenous feed of puréed extreme horror and Absinthe infused sticky-spiced unicorn wings. His anguished cries for help can be found via 365 Tomorrows, Breachzine, AntipodeanSF, Horror Without Borders, Black Hare Press and HellBound books. Hari was the Winner of the Australasian Horror Writers' Association [AHWA] Flash Fiction Award 2018 and has, also, succeeded in being a New Zealander who now lives in Northern Italy with no cats.

Amazon: amazon.com/Hari-Navarro
Tumblr: harinavarro.tumblr.com/

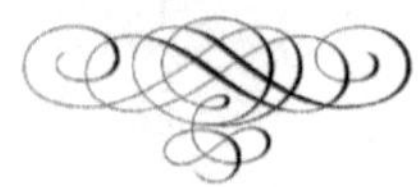

J.W. GARRETT

J.W. Garrett has been writing in one form or another since she was a teenager. She writes speculative fiction from the sunny beaches of Florida, but loves the mountains of Virginia where she was born. Her writings include novels as well as short stories and poetry. Since completing Remeon's Crusade, the third book in her sci-fi fantasy series, Realms of Chaos, she has been hard at work on the next installment, scheduled to release in 2021. When she's not hanging out with her characters, her favorite activities are reading, running and spending time with family.

Website: www.jwgarrett.com
BHC Press: www.bhcpress.com/Author_JW_Garrett.html

JACQUELINE MORAN MEYER

Jacqueline Moran Meyer is a writer, artist and small business owner living in New York, where she received her master's degree from Teachers College, Columbia University. Jacqueline enjoys writing speculative fiction and horror stories. Her favorite author is Alice Munro and her favorite film…is…anything horror related. Jacqueline also enjoys hiking with her dog Molly and the company of her husband Bruce and daughters; Julia, Emma and Lauren. Jacqueline's Mantra lately; WTF.

Website: jmoranmeyer.net
Amazon: www.amazon.com/author/jacquelinemoranmeyer

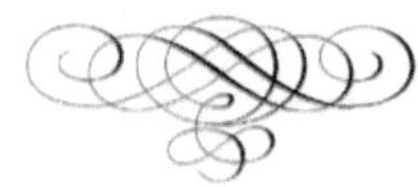

JODI JENSEN

Jodi Jensen, author of time travel romances and speculative fiction short stories, grew up moving from California, to Massachusetts, and a few other places in between, before finally settling in Utah at the ripe old age of nine. The nomadic life fed her sense of adventure as a child and the wanderlust continues to this day. With a passion for old cemeteries, historical buildings and sweeping sagas of days gone by, it was only natural she'd dream of time traveling to all the places that sparked her imagination.

Twitter: @WritesJodi
Facebook: jodijensenwrites

K.B. ELIJAH

K.B. Elijah is a fantasy author living in Brisbane, Australia with her husband and three cockatiels. A lawyer by day, and a writer by...also day, because she needs her solid nine hours of sleep per night (not that the cockatiels let her sleep past 6am). K.B. writes for various international anthologies, and her work features in dozens of collections about the mysterious, the magical and the macabre. Her own books of short fantasy novellas with twists, The Empty Sky and Out of the Nowhere, are available on paperback and Kindle now.

Website: www.kbelijah.com
Instagram: k.b.elijah

KELLY MATSUURA

Kelly Matsuura writes diverse YA, fantasy, and literary fiction. She is the creator of The Insignia Series' anthologies (Asian fantasy themed) and has had stories published with Ink & Locket Press, A Murder of Storytellers, Black Hare Press, and many more. Kelly lives in Nagoya, Japan with her geeky husband. She loves traveling, knitting, cooking, and of course, reading.

Website: www.blackwingsandwhitepaper.com

L.B. ZINGER

L.B. Zinger is the pen name of a retired physician and ethicist. After years of teaching, writing and editing for medical publications, she has decided to attempt to write the stories that have been circling in her head for many years. She is active in her local writing group with an interest in many different genres (except romance).

LYNDSEY ELLIS-HOLLOWAY

Lyndsey Ellis-Holloway is a writer from Knaresborough, UK. She writes fantasy, sci-fi, horror and dystopian stories, focussing on compelling characters and layering in myth and legend at every opportunity. Her mind is somewhat dark and twisted, and she lives in perpetual hope of owning her own Dragon someday, but for now she writes about them to fill the void... and to stop her from murdering people who annoy her. When she's not writing she spends time with her husband, her dogs and her friends enjoying activities such as walking, movies, conventions and of course writing for fun as well!

Website: theprose.com/LyndseyEH

M. SYDNOR JR.

M. Sydnor Jr. is an author of novels and short stories. He began his career in writing in 2005 after trading in his basketball sneakers for a pen and pad, and the desire to create worlds took off. Early in his writing journey, he learned there was more than just putting an idea to paper, you had to read. He lives in Northern California collecting an unhealthy number of movies, books and graphic novels. The characters of his fantasy series, The Legends of the World, take most of his time when he's not coaching high school basketball.

MAJANKA VERSTRAETE

Majanka Verstraete studied law and criminology, and now works as Legal Counsel. Writing has been her passion ever since she learned how to read. She writes about all things supernatural, her books ranging from children's picture books to young adult novels, all the way to new adult academy and reverse harem books.

Website: majankaverstraete.com

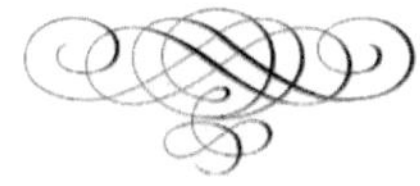

MAXINE CHURCHMAN

Maxine Churchman lives in Essex UK and has recently started writing poetry and short stories to share. Her interests include learning to improve her writing, reading, knitting, walking and teaching yoga. She is also planning a novel.

MICHELLE ANN KING

Michelle Ann King is a speculative fiction writer from Essex, England. Her work has appeared in over ninety different venues, including Interzone, Strange Horizons, and Orson Scott Card's Intergalactic Medicine Show. She has published two collections of short stories, available in ebook and paperback from Amazon and other online retailers, and is currently at work on her third.

Website: www.transientcactus.co.uk

NICOLA CURRIE

Nicola Currie is from Cambridge, UK where she works in educational publishing. She has published poetry in literary magazines, including Mslexia and Sarasvati, and short stories in various anthologies. She has also completed her first novel, which was longlisted for the Bath Children's Novel Award.

Website: writeitandweep.home.blog

RAVEN CORINN CARLUK

Raven Corinn Carluk writes dark fantasy, paranormal romance, and anything else that catches her interest. She's authored five novels, where she explores themes of love and acceptance. Her shorter pieces, usually from her darker side, can be found in Black Hare Press anthologies, at Detritus Online, and through Alban Lake Publishers.

Twitter: @ravencorinn
Website: www.ravencorinncarluk.com

S.O. GREEN

S.O. Green lives in the Kingdom of Fife with husband, John. They have been published in short story anthologies by Otter Libris, Rogue Blades and Dragon Soul Press. They also won 3rd Place in the British Fantasy Society's Short Story Contest 2018 for the feminist post-Apocalypse piece, 'Travesty'. Writer, vegan, martial artist, gamer, occasionally a terrible person (but only to fictional people). They thrive on the unusual, which might explain why there are so many cats.

Website: https://thebasementoflove.blogspot.com/
Twitter:@SOGreenWriter

STEPHEN HERCZEG

Stephen Herczeg is an IT Geek based in Canberra Australia. He has been writing for over twenty years and has completed a couple of dodgy novels, sixteen feature length screenplays and numerous short stories and scripts. His horror work has featured in Sproutlings, Hells Bells, Below the Stairs, Trickster's Treats #1 and #2, Shades of Santa, Behind the Mask, Beyond the Infinite; The Body Horror Book, Anemone Enemy, Petrified Punks and Beginnings. He has also had numerous Sherlock Holmes stories published through the Belanger Books—Sherlock Holmes anthologies.

Amazon: amazon.com/-/e/B07916SQQS
Facebook: stephenherczegauthor

TIM MENDEES

Tim Mendees is a horror writer from Macclesfield in the North-West of England that specialises in cosmic horror and weird fiction. He has had over fifty stories accepted for publication in anthologies and magazines with publishers all over the world, and has two novellas, Miracle Growth (Black Hare Press) and Burning Reflection (Mannison Press), coming soon. When he is not arguing with the spellchecker, Tim is a goth DJ, crustacean and cephalopod enthusiast, and the presenter of a popular web series of live video readings of his material. He currently lives in Brighton & Hove with his pet crab, Gerald, and an army of stuffed octopods.

Website: https://timmendeeswriter.wordpress.com/
You Tube: https://tinyurl.com/timmendeesyoutube

XIMENA ESCOBAR

Ximena is writing stories and poetry. Originally from Chile, she is the author of a translation into Spanish of the Broadway Musical "The Wizard of Oz", and of an original adaptation of the same, "Navidad en Oz", both produced in her home country. Since 2018 she has published several short stories in various anthologies and online platforms, and is now slowly working on her own collection. Ximena has a degree in Arts & Communication Science and lives in Nottingham with her family.

Facebook: Ximenautora
Twitter: @laximenin

ZOEY XOLTON

Zoey Xolton is an Australian Speculative Fiction Author. She likes to daydream, and write stories about the beautiful and improbable, the dark and fantastical, as well as the adventurous and utterly romantic! Whether it's fairy tales, fantasy, horror, paranormal romance, urban fantasy, or science-fiction…she dabbles in it. Zoey has featured in over 100 anthologies to date, and is currently working on progressively longer stories. She prays you enjoy, and fall in love with the deliciously tempting tales, and the characters that she brings into the world. Writing is Zoey's guilty pleasure…perhaps reading her work will become one of yours?

Website: www.zoeyxolton.com

Greed

Acknowledgements

When we embarked on our Black Hare Press journey back in late 2018, we never envisioned the huge support we'd get from the writing community. We have been truly humbled by the number of submissions we've received (around 3,000 over our first eight publications!) and have loved reading every single one.

So, thank you to everyone who crafted tales just for us—from the tiny tales in our Dark Drabbles series to these sinful tales you have read here in Lust—we thank you from the bottom of our hearts.

To our families and friends, collaborators, random strangers who took pity on us, and everyone who has helped us on the way: we couldn't have done it without you.

And to you, our discerning reader, we and these talented writers did it all for you. We hope you enjoyed these tales, and if you did, don't forget to leave a review.

Thank you all—see you next time.

Love & kisses

Ben & Dean

www.blackharepress.com

Greed